杨文新◎著

Women as Other
D.H. Lawrence's Gender Study in Lady
Chatterley's Lover

劳伦斯笔下女性的
他者角色研究

以《查特莱夫人的情人》为例

只有康妮是他的理想女性

一个在他的乌托邦世界存在的"真正女性"他者

一个在他新的男权秩序下存在的"母鸡般温顺的女人"

人民日报出版社

图书在版编目（CIP）数据

劳伦斯笔下女性的他者角色研究：以《查特莱夫人的情人》为例 /
杨文新著 . —北京：人民日报出版社，2018.4
ISBN 978 - 7 - 5115 - 5354 - 6

Ⅰ. ①劳… Ⅱ. ①杨… Ⅲ. ①劳伦斯（Lawrence，David Herbert 1885
- 1930）—小说研究 Ⅳ. ①I561.074

中国版本图书馆 CIP 数据核字（2018）第 043479 号

书　　名：劳伦斯笔下女性的他者角色研究：以《查特莱夫人的情人》为例
作　　者：杨文新

出 版 人：董　伟
责任编辑：刘晴晴
封面设计：中联学林

出版发行：人民日报出版社
社　　址：北京金台西路 2 号
邮政编码：100733
发行热线：（010）65369509　65369846　65363528　65369512
邮购热线：（010）65369530　65363527
编辑热线：（010）65363105
网　　址：www. peopledailypress. com
经　　销：新华书店
印　　刷：三河市华东印刷有限公司

开　　本：710mm×1000mm　1/16
字　　数：150 千字
印　　张：10.5
印　　次：2018 年 5 月第 1 版　　2018 年 5 月第 1 次印刷

书　　号：ISBN 978 - 7 - 5115 - 5354 - 6
定　　价：45.00 元

Acknowledgements

First, I would like to give my thanks to all the leaders and teachers in Dehong Teachers' College where I have worked, who support for my study and work. Without them, I can not have had the opportunity to write the book.

Second and for most, I am grateful to my supervisor, Professor Liu Hanyu, who has patiently tutored me in preparing and writing the first draft of the book. Without her encouragement and insightful instruction, this book would not have reached its present form.

Thirdly, my special thanks are to all my teachers in Yunnan Normal University, Prof. Yuan Yichuan, He Changyi, Li Changyin, Hao Guilian and Yan Kui, including my supervisor and teacher, Prof. Liu Hanyu. Their enlightening teachings and inspiring thoughts in class are of great benefit to my study and completion of the book.

Besides, I want to thank my best friend, Wang Wei, for helping me collect the related materials in Beijing library.

Finally, I would show my sincere thanks to my beloved family. Without their constant support throughout my writing, I could not finish all the chapters of the book.

i

Abbreviations

For the *Fantasia*   *Fantasia of the Unconscious and Psychoanalysis and the Unconscious* by D. H. Lawrence.

LEA   *Late Essays and Articles* by D. H. Lawrence. ed.
James T. Boultion
LCL   *Lady Chatterley's Lover* by D. H. Lawrence

Preface

D. H. Lawrence is one of the twentieth-century's most controversial novelists. His writing often narrates sex between men and women with his philosophy or ideas derived from his experiences. His ideas on duality and ambivalent attitudes on two sexes evoke the fierce arguments between them.

His last novel, *Lady Chatterley's Lover* can be said his complete declaration to the world. In the novel, he continues to develop his doctrine of "stellar equilibrium" into "phallus marriage". For him, man and woman who are like two separate poles can enjoy orgasm simultaneously in the unison with the cosmos by sex as long as the female obeys the male's will and way in body and mind. Obviously, Lawrence's patriarchal ideas which exist in his writing and his understanding of gender roles is based on patriarchal metaphysics of presence. However, there are still many criticisms on tautological replications of Lawrence's own terminology and subversive remarks, which are threatening and destroying gender equality. They argue that the meaning of Lawrence's "phallus" is to preach the mysterious power of life, of love and tenderness, and of androgyny but not of man. In fact, the very expression, the equivalence he sets up between 'sexual' and 'phallic', constitutes sufficient proof. In order to further explore Lawrence's view on gender in *LCL*, an analysis on all the female characters is necessary, for most criticisms less analyzed other female characters, only focusing on the protagonists — Clifford, Connie and Mellors, their triangular relationship and their symbolic meanings.

Employing Beauvoir's "woman as Other for and by men" and Dale Spender's "patriarchal order" in language, the book will analyze the identities of the five women in the novel and find out Lawrence's gender equality further with his philosophy, background and late essays. Through the analysis, Connie's mother, Hilda and Bertha with strong female will against men belong to the type of "cocksure woman" as Other for men in Lawrence's patriarchal order. They disobey femininity and are disliked by their husbands. In Lawrence's patriarchal order, they are not "true women", pursuing equal gender roles separately in society, spirit and sexuality. Mrs. Bolton and Connie, faithful to the patriarchal order, are willing to be the absolute Other by men. However, Mrs. Bolton's social identity at the end of novel is satirized by the author who unreasonably arranges her to accept actively the sexual order and touch of Clifford and tactfully substitutes the role as his mistress for her social identity. Only Connie is his ideal woman, a "true woman" in his utopian world, a "hensure woman" in his new patriarchal order. In his order, female identities should be limited to the traditional identities—be lover, wife and mother at home. She can accept education, can enjoy free love and also can have sexual experiences before marriage, but she must play the role the man ask her to play, faithful to the Father principle, faithful to the patriarchal order. She should do her duty like a "hen" as an absolute Other by men but not try in vain to be a "cock" as Other for men. Based on the conclusion, the end of the thesis will try to further discuss the present problems of gender equality and suggest man and woman should cooperate and build win-win relationship but not conflict to balance the two sexes by Lawrence.

Nowadays, men and women are equal in law, but it does not means men and women are really equal in people's ideologies, behaviors, customs and cultures, etc. It has a long way for women to struggle for equalities of gender's development and status, which needs us to accept the eduction of gender equality, to do and insist on it generation after generation.

Yang Wenxin

May, 2017

前　言

　　戴维德·赫伯特·劳伦斯是二十世纪最具争议的小说家之一。他的写作常常将来自个人经历的哲学思想融入男女之爱的描述中。他双重性的思想及对两性的矛盾态度激起了两性之间激烈的争论。他最后一部小说《查特莱夫人的情人》，可以说是他对这个世界的一个完整宣言。

　　在小说中，他延续发展了他的"星际平衡"原则——"菲勒斯婚姻"。对他而言，男人和女人就像各不相关的两极，只要女性在身体和精神上遵从男性的意志和方式，那么双方就可以通过性交同时达到高潮，与宇宙共鸣。他的作品明显存在男权至上的思想，不难看出他对性属角色的理解是建立在男权形而上的基础之上的。然而，许多关于对劳伦斯的用词同义反复的评论和颠覆性言论却一直在威胁和破坏着性属的平等。他们认为劳伦斯的"菲勒斯"是在宣扬生活的神秘力量，是爱和温柔的力量，是双性同体而不是男性的力量。有些学者用"菲勒斯"替换性爱一词本身已经说明问题。为进一步挖掘劳伦斯在该小说中所持的性属观点，仅仅关注三个主角，克里夫、康妮和梅勒斯及其三角关系和他们所代表的象征意义是远远不够的，需要对小说的所有女性角色进行分析。然而，多数评论对其他女性角色很少提及。

　　因此,该书借用波伏娃和黛儿·斯彭德女性主义观点,即把"女性他者和他者中的他者女性"①和"语言中男权秩序"前后结合,从劳伦斯的哲学思想、个人背景和他后期的文章,来分析小说中五位女性角色的身份认同,以此探讨劳伦斯对于性属所持的观点。通过分析得出,康妮的母亲、希尔达和贝莎都带有反男性的强烈女性意志,属于劳伦斯男权秩序下男人眼里的女性他者,即"公鸡般自负的女人"。她们都违背了女性气质,都被她们的丈夫讨厌,都不是劳伦斯男权秩序下"真正的女性";她们都分别追求着在社会、精神和性领域中的性属平等。而波尔顿太太和康妮都忠实于男权秩序,自愿做男人眼中的绝对他者。然而,波尔顿太太的社会身份认同在小说的结局却遭到了劳伦斯的嘲讽。他不合理地安排她积极接受克利福德的性命令和性接触,巧妙地将她的社会身份认同变成了克利福德的情人。只有康妮是他的理想女性,一个在他的乌托邦世界中存在的"真正女性"他者,一个在他新的男权秩序下存在的"母鸡般温顺的女人"。在他的秩序中,女性身份认同应该局限于传统身份认同——在家做情人、妻子和母亲。她可以接受教育,可以享受自由恋爱,也可以在婚前有性行为,但她必须扮演男人让她扮演的角色,忠实于父性原则和男权秩序。她应该履行她作为"母鸡"的职责,做一个被男人视为绝对他者的女性(他者中

----

① 原英文是"woman as Other for and by men"。笔者在原稿上曾译作"对和被男性视作他者的女性",总觉不通,但又不知道该如何更好地用中文翻译出波伏娃的这个概念。广西师范大学副教授王美萍在评阅原稿后也认为此译法拗口;笔者的恩师,云南师范大学李昌银教授在离校前也建议我一定要坚持斟酌、完善这个译文,让它更能表意。笔者一直思考这个问题,现根据波伏娃的理论内容所指及目前大家对他者理论的接受,将此概念译作"女性他者和他者中的他者女性"。因女性他者是长期男权思想对女性属性强制规范或干预下反抗的女性,她们被男性视为异类;而臣服于男权思想,失去主动性,完全无意识成为男性语言象征体系下的女性,不过是"被创造出来"的,与"反抗"的女性他者相区别,她们其实是又一他者,故有此译。

的他者)而不能妄图做一只"公鸡",一个男人眼里的"他者女性"。基于对五位女性的分析讨论,该研究试图进一步对当前的性属平等问题展开讨论,并提出男人和女人的和谐发展应当建立合作、双赢关系,而不是劳伦斯所主张的通过争斗理论来平衡两性关系。

如今,法律面前男女平等,但法律的男女平等却不等于思想意识、行为习惯、文化等方面的真正平等,女性要实现平等的性属发展和地位上的平等,还有很长的路要走。这个过程,需要一代又一代人对性属平等教育的接受、行动和坚持。

杨文新

2017 年 5 月

Comments on the Study

学术评语:

该论文分析了作品中的性属平等等问题,具有一定的学术价值和现实意义,且综述全面、准确。

该论文显示出作者已具备相应的理论基础和专业知识,分析方法科学,引证资料丰富,具有一定的研究深度。可见,作者已基本具备了独立从事科研的能力。

该研究是对劳伦斯男权秩序思想的深刻解读和对作品中女性形象的全面分析,具有一定的理论意义和现实意义。

郑月莉
河北师范大学副教授评阅
2013 年 4 月

　　论文从女性主义视角分析了《查特莱夫人的情人》中作者劳伦斯的男权至上的思想。

　　论文在选题和立意上都显现出了优秀论文所具有的积极辩论性，一反传统评论对劳伦斯"星际平衡"两性关系的赞同。本论文鲜明地指出劳伦斯的"星际平衡"实为"菲勒斯婚姻"，观点明确，选题具有较高的学术价值。只是，论文中文题目略为拗口。

　　论文主要分析了作品里的五位女性人物，指出劳伦斯的男权思想在对这五位女性人物两分化的刻板描写中显露无遗，一类是挑战男性权威的"公鸡"女人，一类是顺从男性的"母鸡"女人。

　　论文层次分明，论述充分，语言表达流畅，尽管论文在理解劳伦斯两性关系上还存在一定的偏颇，但论文思路清晰，论据翔实，不失为一篇比较优秀的论文。

王美萍

广西师范大学外国语学院副教授评阅

2013 年 5 月

目 录
CONTENTS

Chapter One Introduction

David Herbert Lawrence (1885 – 1930) is a prolific writer of the twentieth century. During more than two decades of his writing, there are 14 novels (including 3 versions of *Lady Chatterley*) , over 60 tales, 11 complete volumes of poetry, 10 plays and 14 non-fiction books (Popawski 211 – 214). He is highly claimed not only as a novelist, novella and short writer, but also as a poet, essayist, translator, dramatist and painter. When compared to Ezra Pound, T. S. Eliot, James Joyce and Virginia Woolf, Lawrence's position on the literary map " at times, seemed far less secure than them" (Fernihough, "introduction" 3). In his books and essays, he expressed freely his extreme ideas on politics, marriage, society, education, religion and man and woman, often by narrating sexuality. So "everyone feels the need, at the outset, either to like him or to dislike him" (Torgovnick 33).

To those who like him, he is a genius, prophet and cultural icon. E. M. Forster calls him the greatest novelist of his generation. F. R. Leavis devotes all his life to supporting him, making him become the 'canon' of English literature and appear with increasing frequency in school and university curricula in the 1950s (Fernihough, "introduction" 4). Later, Raymond Williams and Richard Hoggart from proletarian backgrounds view him as "the sole working-class hero of modern English literature" (Baldick 263).

To those who dislike him, he is one of the most controversial writers. As Eliot sums up, "Lawrence's life as a story of spiritual pride, emotional sickness, self-deception, and a kind of ignorance that would not have been remedied by an Oxbridge grooming" (qtd. in Baldick 257). Feminists also attacks him more bitterly not only for his statement in a letter that his work for women would be "better than the suffrage", but also for the misogyny of much of his work (qtd. in Milne 200). Meanwhile, as a twentieth-century writer, Lawrence was and is usually seen as being marginal to the modernism, for those so-called mainstream writers like James Joyce and Virginia Woolf were almost uniformly hostile or condescending to him, but his apparently marginal position promotes him to "critically central" writer (Bell 179).

Thanks to his unique position in literature, the studies on him and his works since his death have never been reduced, which have become an enormous library of literary-critical writing about him (Baldick 225). Until now, there are over 650 books or pamphlets on him and literally thousands of essays (Paul 274). To the point, Eliot points out earlier, "the books about him give the impression that he is a man to read about, rather than an author to read" (220). The reason lies in Lawrence's works which always mix with his experiences and his philosophy together. They are like a set of triplet.

1. 1   Lawrence's Triplet（Experiences, philosophy and Works）—Pursuing the Significance of Male

Critics agree that Lawrence's background or experiences are still the raw material of his writing. He was born in a working-class family. His father was an illiterate coal miner and his mother was a teacher. Growing up in a mining village named Eastwood, he hated the mines. The scenes about environmental pollution and human mechanization caused by industrial civilization are frequently repeated in his works.

Apart from it, his parents' relationship is also the key element to influence himself and his writing. His mother, Lydia Beardsall, was a daughter of an engineer from a middle-class family. She had taught school. Her husband, Lawrence's father was a miner, hot-tempered, unschooled, and robust. He "hated books, hated the sight of anyone reading or writing", while she hated "the thought that any of her sons should be condemned to manual labour. Her sons must have something higher than that" (*Studies in Classic American Literature* 125). They almost had little in common, which made their marriage disastrous. To them, Lawrence has complicated emotions. First, he loves and depends on her mother but hates his father. Then, he gradually likes his father and tries to escape the control and influence of his mother, just like his autobiographical novel, *Sons and Lovers.* For him, his mother is always a "cocksure woman" in terms of his division on women (*LEA* 125 – 127). Thus, Lawrence loves her mother but fears her and wants to escape her, which also influences his attitudes on other women. On the one hand, he dislikes those possessive women or "cocksure women"; on the other hand, he feels that they are more powerful than men (Frieda 55). In his writings, the relationship between man and woman, often in marriage, is still what he tried his best to explore. Generally speaking, his parents' marriage was disastrous but "produced D. H. Lawrence" (Murry B.).

His sexual experiences about his lovers or female friends like Jessie Chambers, Louie Burrows and Alice Dax etc, and especially his wife, Frieda, greatly influenced his writing too. Because of his long-termed repressed sexuality by his unchallenged mother and Christianity, after reading Darwin and Nietzsche at university, sex is a new experience for young him (Gao 59; Priest 58). Through it, he succeeds in unloading the obsessional emotions to his mother and starts to search independently for "who am I, sexually speaking?" (Torgovnick 33). That's why he pays so much attention to sex in his whole writing. Through sex, he interprets the meaning of man and woman or gender originally.

Moreover, influenced by the Great War and the battles of the two sexes in his age, he always " traced the origins of human destructiveness to *the desire for mastery*— over nature, over the body, over one's mate, over servant classes and rival nations and whatever appears to resist the personal or collective will" (Sander 135). His illness, pulmonary tuberculosis is also partly forced him to explore the related dual death-rebirth theme. As Sander points out that this quest for mastery above, according to Lawrence, is founded upon the illusion of separation: the illusion that mind can be divorced from body, self from other, humanity from nature. The attitude of domination presupposes a master and something else to be mastered (135).

What he held on are written into his novels and books, which also formed his own philosophy. Though he did not write a book on his philosophy, his ideas on it are developed in his works. He says:

> It seems to me it was the greatest pity in the world, when philosophy and fiction got split. They used to be one, right from the days of the myth... So the novel went sloppy, and philosophy went abstract—dry. The two should come together again—in the novel (Lawrence, *Phoenix* 520).

Many critics have noticed that he liked the method of stating every question in terms of the opposition of two contraries (Potter 24). In *Twilight in Italy* (1916), he writes, "the consummation of man is twofold, in the Self and in Selflessness" (qtd. in Dalski 5). And in *Reflections on the Death of a Porcupine* (1925), he directly proclaimed his own duality, "I know I am compounded of two waves, I, who am temporal and mortal... I am framed in the struggle and embrace of the two opposite waves of darkness and of light" (24). He even believes that "everything that exists, even a stone, has two sides to his nature" (183). To him, the universe consists of opposing principles. These opposites are in continuous conflict but complementary at the same time. The equilibrium between them can only last so long as these conflicting yet complementary elements exist.

Duality is still his main characteristic of his ideas. To gender roles, he first writes in *the Study of Thomas Hardy*, "[e]very man comprises male and female in his being, the male always struggling for predominance. A woman likewise consists in male and female, with female predominant" (481). According to many bibliographical books, Lawrence liked the housewifely virtues, cooking, scrubbing sewing and the making of clothes

（Moore 161）. He was shy, decent and tender, preferring girls to stay with. Many critics agree that, his novels are always reconciling the male and female elements in himself. Some of them even argue that he is a woman. Norman Mailer, in his *The Prisoner of Sex*（1971）responded that "Lawrence, despite his temporary deviation into the cult of phallic mastery, was a true worshiper of women, and indeed understood them as no other writer had done before, partly because he was spiritually female himself" （qtd. in Baldick 266）. Carol Dix has the similar view of him as a kind of woman writer hidden under a masculine appearance（Baldick 266）.

In fact, his concept is very similar to Woolf's "androgyny", which is controversial in feminists. To Showalter, it "represents as escape from the confrontation with femaleness or maleness（241）", while to Toril Moi, it means "the goal of the feminist struggle must precisely be to deconstruct the death-dealing binary oppositions of masculinity and femininity"（237）. Time testifies the truth. Along with the development of gender studies, it is known that gender roles are rooted in culture but not biological sexes. Lawrence and Woolf, as the writers of the twentieth century, seemed not to explain the question. So they believed that humans could be "woman-manly or man-womanly"（Showalter, 241）.

At their age, the idea can be said reasonable and progressive. But later, he changed it in *the Study of Thomas Hardy* and became extreme. That's why feminists and many other male critics do not agree with Norman Mailer and Carol Dix, for Lawrence did not succeed in reconciling the female and male elements in himself, on the contrary, pursued the absolute significance of male in writing.

His novels can prove the point. His early works, *The White Peacock*

(1911), *the Trespasser* (1912) and *Sons and Lovers* (1913) only shows the experiences of his youth and the problems associated with his relationship with his father and mother. They are immature. During the period, he was only "the eternal mamma's boy" (Ruderman 249). But since *The Rainbow* (1915), he started constructing his own ideas on man and woman based on his experiences in marriage with his wife, Frieda. Frieda, mature and intellectual, had been a wife and mother before meeting him. She, influenced deeply by Otto Gross, a disciple of Freud, believed that "if only sex were 'free' the world would straight— away turn into a paradise" (3). In travelling with Lawrence, she took off her clothes and danced around him in the room (Priest 58 +). The similar scene repeatedly appears in *Rainbow*, *Sun* (1925, short story) and *LCL*. Compared to mature wife, young Lawrence was shocked by her open sexuality. Strangely, she was also a "cocksure woman" like his mother but he married her. According to his letters, he needed her difference to arise the quarrels between them, which could help his genius in writing (Gao 67).

It is obvious that his experiences influence his novels but also his philosophy. In *The Rainbow*, though he argues "two in one", he feels the expansion of feminine existence is a threat to masculine existence. He believes, in marriage, if men can not conquer women in their intellects or spirits, men should satisfy them in bed at least. If the latter is also a failure, women defeat men in sex, and then men will be destroyed completely.

To pursue the wholeness of male, in *Women in Love* (1920), he changed from "two in one" to "stellar equilibrium", or "unison in separateness". According to his "stellar equilibrium", male and female should never seek the position of domination in sex and use one's sex as tool of the will or that's the fatal mistake; one must break the barriers of the ego, give up all personality and then transcend the limits of consciousness. In that case, each member of the couple can keep a complete being, perfectly polarized. When one feels assured in his virility, and the other in her femininity, the sexual act is a marvelous fulfillment of each one by the other. Beauvoir points out, the idea is "not for him to define the special relations of woman and of man, but to restore both of them to the verity of Life" (245). However, the practice of the idea lying in the sexual relationship between Birkin and Ursula can not make readers and some critics convinced. His abstract and symbolic narration of sex confuses them on the contrary. Jeffrey Meyers and Wilson Knight doubt the sex act between Birkin and Ursula may be "anal intercourse", not the normal intercourse (Gao 247).

In fact, as Beauvoir points out, on the one hand Lawrence argues that masculine arrogance provokes feminine resistance and only "the reign of mutuality" without domination between man and woman can reach to the perfect balance; on the other hand, he fails to construct the reign. The heroine obeys the idea of the hero and is conquered and saved by him (247 – 248).

In the third period, Lawrence entered the other extreme to explore further the theme of male wholeness. In the works of *Aaron's Rod* (1922), *Kangaroo* (1923) and *The plumed Serpent* (1926), the male is the hero and leader in the world of men who denies the right of a woman to enter the world and in the realm of personal relations, demands her complete submission to him. The period is said to be the worst of his writing, showing the decline in artistic achievement. In fact, these works thoroughly express his patriarchal philosophy in *the Fantasia*. As Murry J. Middleton points out that, he wants to solve his problem or the great problem of our day, "how to regain innocence in sex" and " change the world of men that in future no child shall be compounded, and conditioned, and compelled as he was" (346 – 348). In the period, he has given up what he said in the *Study of Thomas Hardy*. His argument on gender roles has been changed as follows:

> A child is either male or female, in the whole of its psyche and physique is e-
> ther male or female. Every single living cell is either male or female, and will
> remain either male or female as long as life lasts. And every single cell in every
> male child is male, and every cell in every female child is female (*F* 96).

In this period, he believes, the "vital sex polarity" is "dynamic magic of life" (F 103). Daleski points out it shows "a deep split in Lawrence himself " (11). The split is first derived from the different influence of his parents on him and then of his wife. Besides, after experiencing the World War and feminist movements, he splited more seriously. For women's gai-ning higher status in society and working outside and men's horror and pas-siveness in the situation made him believe that the roles of two sexes were inverted, which was neither natural nor healthy for the society. This is a "perverted process" (F 141).

To explain the differences between man and woman, he argues that man is active as "thinker and doer" while woman is passive as "the initia-tor of emotion" (F 97). For him, when men discover their emotions from women, women only learn how to think or at least how to work their minds from men (F 102). Besides, he defines the roles of men and women in all areas of life. He believes that their own roles are distinct in every aspect of life from education to marriage and this distinction should be created at the very early stages of life. He argues that girls and boys should be educated separately and differently. He proposes that girls should be educated for domestic arts, and boys should be educated to be individuals. This segregation in education aims to prevent girls from being "self-conscious" and make them conscious of the sacredness of their home, and make boys aware of their "manly rule" (*F* 87). In marriage, women should be submissive and men dominant. Women's submission should be "an instinctive, unconscious submission, made in unconscious faith. " (*F* 196). Furthermore, Lawrence claims that a man's world is outside, dealing with abstract issues while "woman for him exists only in the twilight [···] Evening and the night are hers. " (*F* 109). For him, women should exist as men's sexual mates of the home.

According to the *study of Hardy*, *the Fantasia* and *Phoenix*, Daleski lists a table as follows to present Lawrence's attributes of male and female.

Male	Female
Activity	Stability, Immutability
Change	Permanence, Eternality
Will-to-Motion	Will -to-Inertia
Knowlege	Feeling, Nature
Timelessness	The Moment
Idea	Body
Doing	being
Abstraction	
Public Good	Enjoyment through the Senses
Community	
Love	Law

续表

Spirit	Soul
Consciousness	Feelings
Mind	Senses
Son	Father
action	Feeling, Emotion
Stalk	Root
Light	Darkness
Movement towards discovery	Movement towards origin
Abstracted and Mechanical Life	Personal Life
Volitional Centres	Sympathetic Centres
Authority	Gentle, All – Sympathetic Role
Active	Passive
Initiator	Responder
Utterance	Emotion
Doing and Thinking	Procreation
Assertion	Hesitation
Insentient	Sensitive
Fealess, Relentless Heroism	Altruistic Endurance
Responsibility	Tenderness
Disinterested, Non – Domestic	
Purpose	Feeling

(*"The Duality of Lawrence"* 9)

From the table above, we can see that Lawrence extremely emphasizes "an absolute degree of masculinity" (Daleski 11). These attributes of male and female are obviously based on the ideas of patriarchy he takes for granted. For him, men and women are born different.

Obviously, his philosophy is not scrupulous, not only metaphysical but also even contradictory. "Father" in female principle often misleads the male critics, such as Mr. Hough who argues that "Lawrence is not constructing the world on the model of sexual duality. The father, for example, is on the same side as the female" (qtd. in Daleski 10). In fact, the Father is that manifestation of God which personifies female values (Daleski10). For him, as long as the female accepts the Father, their ideas and behaviors will be "in unconscious faith" to men. The principle has constituted the sufficient proof that his gender roles are based on patriarchal metaphysics of presence (Akgun 21). Besides, his "(knowing by) body" belongs to the female principle but is very similar to his male "(phallic) consciousness" while his male principle— abstraction, will, spirit or mind—is still what he spent a lot of his life fighting against.

Ironically, he called his philosophy as "pseudo – philosophy" (*F*xiv). He admitted that his ideas were often dynamic and temporary, even contradictory. As Earl Brewster says, when he "urged Lawrence to write at length on his philosophical and psychological conceptions, he shook his head and said: I would contradict myself in every page " (qtd. in Vivas ix).

However, for him, man and woman are still opposite and conflicting yet complementary, just like poles. His wife Frieda explains in *Not I but Wind*, "[Lawrence] felt that each should keep intact his own integrity and isolation, yet at the same time preserve a mutual bond like the north and south poles which between them enclose the world" (vii). In conflicting between man and woman, how to "keep the balance, not to trespass, not to topple over" is one of his chief themes (Frieda vii).

It is obvious that he is not an egalitarian. He believes that it is natural that men master women. If women master men, that's "identity crisis" (Kermode 155). It's why in his philosophy and writing he has contradictory attitudes to women: he wants to balance the relationship between man and woman but as a male writer, he does not correct his patriarchal idea but strengthen it on the contrary. As Simpson points out, " Attacks on Lawrence's misogyny and praise for his sensitive portrayals of femininity have co-existed since the inception of the critical debate" (13).

1.2 *Lady Chatterley's Lover*

In the fourth period, Lawrence wrote three versions of *LCL* from November 1926 to January 1928. Many critics argue that the novel(mainly the third version) is not his masterpiece. F. R. Leavis calls it "a bad novel" with many failures in creative wholeness in the artist (94). Eliseo Vivas also criticizes it as the failure of art because compared to the former works, "Lawrence imitates Lawrence" (3). So does Draper, who argues that the last novels of Lawrence are merely going over what is for him the old ground. Compared to them, Daleski's comment turns moderate, who thinks it is only a little inferior to *The Rainbow* and *Women in Love* (117). However, Lawrence did not think so at all. Though *Lady Chatterley's Lover* is the most notorious of his novels, he "valued it highly as an expression of his message to the world", for he "allowed himself great freedom in his descriptions of sexual congress and love play" (Craig 146). Wilson is the one who praises highly the novel, "it is the most inspiriting book from England that I have seen in a long time,... one of the best written" and "one of his most vigorous and brilliant" (345).

For Lawrence, *LCL* is his last and complete declaration to the world because the novel shows the rich and complicated themes he wants to express freely. "Tenderness, brutality and paralysis, manhood, womanhood, loyalty, response, passion, industrialism, nature and civilization, intellect, urban life, political organization, destruction, how to live" are the themes of the novel. As Rudikoff says, they are not out of date and still related to our life (408 – 409). That's why the novel has been the critical centre in literary.

In the novel, Lawrence continues to develop his dual view and patriarchal philosophy. For him, body has been mastered by mind or will. The dull, abstract, repressed and mechanical mental life has destroyed the body and the self, resulting in the separation of humanity from the nature. These unharmonious relationships have caused self-annihilation of human beings. To keep the vigour of life, he praises the "blood consciousness", "primal consciousness" or "phallic consciousness", which in his eyes can emancipate the real self. Thus, for him, compared to "will", "body" is more real to know the world and "physical contact", "physical labour" and "physical consciousness" are more important to keep humans' vigour than "will". Simply, he believes that "body is wiser than the mind" (Meyers 123).

He also explicitly narrates and praises sex between Lady Chatterley and his husband's gamekeeper, Mellors. For him, sex is the primitive virility in the nature. It's "the anima of natural integration" (Grefor 101). Sex is life, beauty and fire. The true sex appeal is "the communicating of the warmth, the glow of sex" (*LEA* 146). He believes that sex is not ugly and it can bring humans "an added flow of energy and optimism" (*LEA* 148). For him, without an absolute freedom of sexual expression there is no complete emancipation of sex (Zhang 220).

LCL's fate, however, also like Lawrence's, is changeable and fluctua- ted wildly along with the time. It witnessed three historic periods of the reading public, " as pornography, as a contribution to the campaigns against censorship and for civil and sexual liberties, as a counter – case which has energized the feminist cause" (Lyon), but Lyon argues that *LCL* has no di- rect relation to these purposes. The novel is only an idiosyncratic novel. He argues that feminist critics have objected to what they see here as Lawrence's bullying veneration of male sexuality and the phallic imagination; there is some truth in the attack, but Lawrence's treatment of sexuality is too idiosyncratic to be representative of a general male chauvin- ism. He claims that Connie's and Mellors's sexual explorations lead to a moving and largely persuasive affirmation, not of male power, but of the val- ue of touch and tenderness.

Gregor holds the similar idea. He explains, it is in sex, Lawrence feels, that man encounters most fully the awesome mystery of Life itself, that he comes to understand the Power which infinitely transcends him. "It is not a phallic cult but an animistic encounter which lies at the centre of Lawrence's concern with sex" (102).

To their views, the famous feminist, Simone de Beauvoir in her French book, *The Second Sex* (1949), argues that in *LCL*, Lawrence still uses the doctrine of " stellar equilibrium" and develops it broadly into a clearer claim, " phallic marriage" — " the phallus serves as a means of union between two rivers; it conjoins the two different rhythms into a single flow" (qtd. in Beauvoir 248). The claim shows "the man is not only one of the two elements in the couple, but also their connecting factor; he provides their transcendence: 'The bridge to the future is the phallus' " (245). The very expression, the equivalence he sets up between 'sexual' and 'phallic', constitutes sufficient proof. Obviously, his aim is to keep or recreate passionately "the supremacy of the male". To illuminate the sexual nature of the cosmos, he substitutes "a phallic cult" for "the cult of the Goddess Mother" (245 – 248). Moreover, the hero, Mellors, like other heroes of his novels, from the start hold the secret of wisdom; his submission to the cosmos has been accomplished so long since and he derive from it so much inner certainty, he seem as arrogant as any proud individualist; there is a god who speaks through him: Lawrence himself. In the novel, the heroine "is not evil, she is even good— but subordinated". Beauvoir clearly claims, "the ideal of the 'true' woman that Lawrence has to offer us—that is, the woman who unreservedly accepts being defined as the Other" (245 – 254).

The female critics, Porter, Kate Millett and Simpson continue to denounce the phallus worship of the novel. Differently, Simpson also agrees that the novel is "a recoil from the obsession with power and a return to the values of love and gentleness" (Riedel 331 – 333). The male critic Daleski has the contrary conclusions. In 1959, he stated that Lawrence came full circle, "there is a movement away from the hero to 'tenderness' and the ambiguous 'phallic consciousness' is opposed to the 'mental consciousness'. ⋯it is a fully achieved and harmonious whole, the triumphant assertion of the female principle" (18). In 1965, however, Daleski overthrew his conclusion and reargued that in the third period, Lawrence was trying "to establish a new kind of 'male' significance and to assert a desire for male domination" but he wrote so badly, against his own deepest values. Until the last novel, he succeeded in giving full and vivid expression to those values but asserting a covert 'male' significance with the overt 'female' tendency resulted in "its major blemish" (117). Thus about love and gentleness, they indeed belong to the rich themes of the novel but not so successful and obvious as Lawrence defends.

Except these, there are many criticisms as "the tautological replication of Lawrence's own terminology and the ritualistic rehearsing of his prophecies" (Fernihough "introduction" 5) , continuing to propagandize Lawrence's patriarchal ideas and threat to the present gender equality. However, the good news is that like Daleski, some male critics have noticed the problem of Lawrence's patriarchal ideas under the raising influence of feminism and have moved from a extreme support and blind worship into objective and reasonable amendments. Connie's "passivity in sexuality" and "abandoned female will" have accepted by them, such as Daleski, Bedient, Rudikoff, Tindall and Squires (113 – 115; 370; 411 – 413; 356 – 357; 131) . Except Connie, Mellors' denouciation of Bertha Coutts and of women as lesbians also expose Lawrence's fantasy in sexuality without scientific basis—in effect, Lawrence distinguishes clitoral from vaginal orgasm (Squires 131).

In the 21st century, female critics like Fernihough, have entered understanding and appreciating Lawrence's works more comprehensively. However, Cornelis Schulze in *the Battle of the Sexes in D. H. Lawrence's Prose, Poetry and Paintings* (2002) , clearly distance herself from feminist criticism, arguing that the symbol of the phallus, much emphasized by Lawrence, has attained "androgynous qualities, not at all involving violence and subordination" as femi-nists tend to think and appealing readers for allowing "a deeper, a 'whole' un-derstanding of Lawrence's views on women and his changing presentation of the relationship between the sexes", which is "an equilibrium in which the battle of the sexes has been transcended" (106 – 115;298 – 296).

1.3 Significance of the Study

Through the studies above, we can see that there are still many criti-cisms repeating what Lawrence says with his philosophy and without clear judgments; and even some subversive remarks reappear in our days. Those subversive remarks and those tautological replications of Lawrence's own terminology are highly dangerous to build or keep gender equality. To fur-ther explore Lawrence's gender equality bases on patriarchal ideas in *LCL*, an analysis on all the female characters is necessary, for most criticisms of-ten focus on the protagonists—Clifford, Connie and Mellors, their triangular relationship and their symbolic meanings. The criticisms on other female characters are less analyzed; and the feminist studies on Lawrence's gender equality in *LCL* have not been enough yet.

Linking supplementary evidences from Lawrence's experiences, philos-ophy and the late essays and employing "women as Other" for and by men argued by Simone de Beauvoir in *The Second Sex* and "Patriarchal Order" argued by Dale Spender in *Man Made Language*, the book will discuss the identities of the five women. First, Other for men in Lawrence's patriarchal order, including Connie's mother—a "cocksure woman" as Other for men in society, Hilda—a "cocksure woman" as Other for men in spirit and Bertha—a "cocksure woman" as Other for men in sexuality; Second, Other by men in Lawrence's patriarchal order, including Mrs. Bolton— not a "hensure mother" again but as an absolute Other by men in Lawrence's patriarchal order and Connie a "hensure woman" as an absolute Other by men in Lawrence's patriarchal order.

Based on the analysis, the study's findings on gender equality are more comprehensive—in Lawrence's patriarchal order, female identities should be limited to the traditional identities, being lover, wife and mother at home; they should be faithful to the Father principle, faithful to the patriarchal order, being the absolute Other by men. Thus, in the end the book suggests man and woman should cooperate and build win-win relationship but not conflict by Lawrence, which will be more reasonable, feasible and mutually beneficial to balance the relationship between man and woman.

Chapter Two Literature Review

For Lawrence, sex seems a skeleton key to an individual and society. Through narrating sex in detail in *LCL*, he freely expresses his complicated ideas and philosophy in the themes of the novel. As the introduction mentions, duality is Lawrence's characteristic style. In *A Propos of Lady Chatterley's Lover*, he points out:

> In fact, thought and action, word and deed, are two separate forms of consciousness, two separate lives which we lead. We need, very sincerely, to keep a connection. But while think, we do not act, and while we act we do not think. The great necessity is that we should act according to our thoughts, and think according to our acts. ⋯ Yet they should be related in harmony (218).

The real point of the novel, he argues, is to "want men and women to be able to think sex, fully, completely, honestly and cleanly" (217). To him, the reason is that the ancestors have so assiduously acted sex without ever thinking it or realizing it, that now the act tends to be mechanical, dull and disappointing, and only fresh mental realization will freshen up the experience. To make a balance between the consciousness of the body's sensations (think) and experiences (act), he claims that using the so-called obscene words are necessary because these are a natural part of the mind's consciousness of the body. "Obscenity only comes in when the mind despises and fears the body, and the body hates and resists the mind" (217 – 218).

Besides, he states specially the book is good for women because thousands of women in his age "know nothing, they can't think sexually at all; they are morons in this respect. It is better to give all girls this book, at the age of seventeen…" (218). Meanwhile, he argues, "Life is only bearable when the mind and body are in harmony, and there is a natural balance between them, and each has a natural respect for the other" (218).

His propos of *LCL* influence the criticisms on the novel greatly, especially those who support him.

2. 1   International Studies

2. 1. 1   Criticism from Male Critics

Like Lyon and Gregor, many critics interpret the novel often according to Lawrence's propos or philosophy but some, especially after 1960s, argue some amendments to the novel under the influence of feminism. What they most often concerned with the two related themes in the novel are the sexual theme of regeneration through intimate relationships and the other is the social theme of conflict between the vitality of nature and the mechanized order of modern industrial society (*Twentieth-Century Literary Criticism*

Volume 48 91).

In fact, the rich themes of the novel are linked together in order to explore the "tragic age" of the western world after the First World War and how to establish a new world (*LCL* 1). It can be simply called the dual death-rebirth or annihilation-regeneration theme. To fulfill the great theme, Lawrencean "mystical sexual religion" is the only way: " ' regeneration by sex' of England and of the white race" (Undset 353). That is why many male critics support him greatly. To the point, Lawrence is indeed a brilliant writer, who expresses such a high theme on human being's annihilation and regeneration only through individual's sexual experience.

In the novel, he exhibits two opposite worlds to actualize his dual death-rebirth theme. One is a "living-death" world (Miller 336), the Chatterley's world, full of the dull, abstract, utopian and traditional Platonism (Voelker 227 – 228). The world stands for modern England with its passional emptiness and worship of material wealth (Bedient 370). This worship is a way of power to destruction because "power over the mines and the miners, over Connie, over the material universe" lies doom, just like the wars caused by power (Sanders 139). Thus this is a world of violence, full of class-hatred (Kohn 189 +). In the world, the sky is dark or grey. All the people are under a "fume-laden atmosphere" (Moynahan 104). Whether the upper or the lower class, they only live mechanically, even including their sex and labor.

The other is a living world of love and tenderness, Oliver Mellors' world. The world is close to the nature and is a living universe. In such world, "men and woman, like tree, bird, and flower, are physically alive and growing. This is the basic human reality, and all higher possibilities depend upon the healthy condition of the physical man and woman" (Moynahan 103 – 107). In the world, for Lawrence, bodies are our selves and the only way to be alive is the flesh. Though Mellors is from the working class but he is a "natural aristocrat", a gentleman in everything except birth. His background and education allow him to condemn both the destructive industrial capitalism and the world of the disciplined modern masses (Kohn 189). He is a real man with "blood consciousness" or "phallic consciousness". He has no ambition to make money and totally rejects the Chatterley's world. His task is to preserve the wild life of the wood (Daleski 110 – 112).

Many criticisms show Mellors' body is free and his job is physical. Unlike Chatterley or miners restricted by machine, he has passionate sexuality like a wild animal, which is just the mystery of life. Through sex, he warms the "dying" Connie from the Chatterley's world and makes her rebirth as "a true woman". At the same time, Mellors transcends his unhappy past, regenerating a virile man. In the end, Connie decides to leave her husband and stay with Mellors. Her decision is a successful declaration of experiencing a sexual and spiritual rebirth. Their combination and a new being in her womb symbolize a new world in the future. To the point, Wilson praises Lawrence's theme is a high one in 1929 (345). Milne also points out that Lawrence's novels "investigate the moral and existential choices open to individuals in this society, but as a literary form the novel formalizes lived experience as ideological representation" (198).

Among these male critics, some have found some problems in the novel. Daleski points that Lawrence fails to balance "body consciousness" with "mental consciousness" in the novel. His third and final version, *LCL*, shows that " 'a truce' could not be established between the two until the 'mental consciousness' had been decisively routed". Mellors has both "his way" and "his will" of Connie and she has to be a passive and physical slave. Paradoxically, Mellors has the courage of his tenderness but is celebrated as a man of power (111 – 115). Bedient Calvin also finds, to be the beloved, Connie is deprived of personality. Her "self" is "the particular object both of Lawrence's and of Mellors' fear and hatred, so their desire is " not love, not even tenderness, certainly not joy, but organic peace" (370). Tindall concludes that in the stories of Lawrence, enjoying the hero's illustrations, moved by his ideas, the heroine more or less abandons hers (356 – 357).

About tenderness, his best friend, Murry J. Middleton in 1929 first argued that Mellors' tenderness is always "mixed up with a lot of rage"; as Mellors wonders if he really has the courage of his own tenderness, Lawrence " has the tenderness but he has not got the courage of it" (92).

About passion, Rudikoff finds, nothing really happens to Mellors. "Sexually, the novel is concerned with Connie's feelings; Mellors appears as her teacher, already awakened, and not deeply changed by the passion he a-wakes in her" (411). About Clifford and his world, he argues, "Civilization is always renewed; it has never the finality of being concentrated or ended in a single generation, in a single form of life, in a single person" (412 – 413).

Thus Lawrence's utopian world is only a daydream but the Chatterley's world is the world and "it won't disappear," as Melors says in the novel (Bedient 370). All in all, his high theme is not reasonable and successful. As Gregor's criticism says, "Lawrence not only give us no dramatic key to the 'deathly' consciousness of Clifford and the 'vital' consciousness of

Mellors, but that he has got himself into a position where, if the reader thinks in these terms, he misunderstands the whole position" (101).

About Bertha, many critics agree with Lawrence's saying, "a sort of sensual bloom" (*LCL* 149) or "obscene" (Moynahan105). About the abuse and attack on her sexuality and insisting on Connie's passivity in sexual intercourse, Squires argues that "it probably has a biographical origin". In effect, Lawrence distinguishes clitoral from vaginal orgasm. This is related to his wife, Frieda. Through personal experience, he designed his novel partly to teach Frieda how to live with him (131). At the point, Torgovnick also points out, Mellors' denunciation of Bertha Coutts and of women as lesbians in the novel cannot simply be read as part of Lawrence's fear of female sexuality but should be viewed he is in narrating sex not just as mechanical, physical action (42 – 47). Then, this is only Lawrence's fantasy in sexuality, no scientific basis.

About Mrs. Bolton, she is only mentioned in analyzing Clifford. About their kisses and touch in the end, Daleski, John Haegert and Darper P. Ronald view the behavior as a "childish perversity" from the perspective of Clifford (113 ; 77 ; 266 – 267) ; Julian Moynahan thinks they are "in monstrous, unvital embrace" (77) ; and for Dennis Jackson, the sexuality act between Clifford and Mrs. Bolton, on the theme of Connie and Mellors's regeneration provides an "ironic commentary" : Clifford's access to a "strange new sort of potency" as a consequence of Mrs. Bolton's nursing (266 – 267). Doherty Gerald also points out that, "While Mellors' touch anticipates a freshly eroticized world that will refashion the future, Clifford's touch revives an archaic world of sensations that repeats past identifications"—a baby (372).

All in all, through the criticisms above, except Connie, most male critics do not focus on exploring other women in the novel. To Connie, from "sexual regeneration" and "spiritual regeneration" to "passivity in sexuality" and "abandoned female will", the amendments show, under the influence of feminism, some male critics have realized the problem of patriarchal ideas in the novel and themselves. To Bertha, the review on her is only mentioned in analyzing Mellors' sexuality or Lawrence's sexual experience. To Mrs. Bolton, she is only related to Sir Chatterley's final "male hysteria" (*LCL* 218).

2.1.2　Criticism from Female Critics

The Criticism against his ideas is mainly written by the critics from the view of feminism. Most of them are female critics. There are also some female critics supporting Lawrence. Anais Nin in 1932 praised highly *Lady Chatterley's Lover* and the author. She notes, "it is the first time that a man has so wholly and completely expressed woman accurately. " She even thinks, Lawrence "had a complete realization of the feeling of women. In fact, very often he wrote as a woman would write" (348). Her ideas are often quoted by some male critics to attack the feminist criticism on Lawrence.

From the historic background of the novel, Lawrence was not the only one talking about sex. Psychoanalytical theorists such as Freud and Jung, saw repressed sexual energy everywhere; sexologists such as Havelock Ellis, whose most famous work is *The Psychology of Sex* (1897 – 1928), was greatly responsible for changing British and American attitudes toward sexuality (Ellis 558); and first-wave feminists and educators such as Marie

Stopes, campaigned for contraception and sex education for women. Her book *Married Love* (1918) articulated the new goal of sex within marriage: not conception but simultaneous orgasm (Priest 58). However, it was Lawrence who "narrated sex" in literary (Torgovnick 47). His contemporaries also wrote about sex, such as Joyce whose *Ulysses* is also in the popular charge of obscenity, but he employs the stream of consciousness to represent sex not "a visionary experience" like Lawrence (Cowan 140 – 145).

To the point, the novel is indeed original but as the former amendments by the male critics show, Lawrence's motivation, writing "guidebooks for women" (Beauvoir 253), is not successful because as a male writer, especially with patriarchal idea, his writing can not really represent female sexuality and guide women how to understand their sexualities.

Beauvoir, in her *Second Sex*, has marked Lawrence's mistake clearly. Except the former criticism argued by her, she also points out, for Lawrence, "It is much more difficult for woman than for man to 'accept the universe', for man submits to the cosmic order autonomously, whereas woman needs the mediation of the male" (253).

Katherine Anne Porter (1960) notes that, in the novel, Lawrence constantly describes what man *did*, but tells readers with great authority what woman *felt*. "It is like a textbook of instruction to a woman as to how she *should* feel in such a situation" (367). She even thinks, Lawrence has "a very deep grained fear and distrust of sex itself; he was never easy on that subject, could not come to terms with it for anything" (367). Edith Sitwell (1965) claims clearly that the novel to her is a very dirty and completely worthless book of no literary importance. Mellors' language is " unutterably filthy, cruel, and smelly speech" but nobody seems to have thrashed

27

him. On the contrary, "more idiotic of the British public" accepted the speech "as being a fine example of the workingman's frank, splendid mode of expression" (369 – 370).

Kate Millett, in *Sexual Politics* (1970), argues that the love between man and woman in Lawrence is set against the distorted human relations under industrialization, but this love is based upon the male sexism. In "the older sexual roles" he pursues, Connie is oppressed both by the material society and patriarchal ethic. She becomes a subordination of Mellors' phallus. Millett claims, Lawrence is a subtle conveyor of a masculine message through a feminine consciousness. She even calls him as "the most talented and fervid of sexual politicians" (238 – 257). Though Millett's political attack with literary representation is a little inadequate, Lawrence as "cultural icon" of a sexual and moral example in the 1960s was knocked off by her book (Milne 204 – 207). For it was the best-known and most influential book of the second-wave feminism. Since then, the reaction to him in public reading changed a lot.

After that, with the development of feminism's opening up into a broader-based and more flexible concept of gender, female critics have started to change their single criticism into more complicated and comprehensive studies on him.

Simpson's *D. H. Lawrence and Feminism* (1982) discusses the three periods of his different attitudes on women. To the last novel, she argues that the concern for power is still apparent in the phallus worship of the last novel. On the other hand, she says, the novel is "a recoil from the obsession with power and a return to the values o f love and gentleness" (Riedel 331 – 333). Her conclusion is contradictory, but as she claims, "[a]ttacks on

Lawrence's misogyny and praise for his sensitive portrayals of femininity have co-existed since the inception of the critical debate" (13).

Later, Carol Siegel, in *Lawrence Among the Women* (1991) , argues that during studying feminist theories on gender difference and setting Lawrence squarely in the center of these discussions, feminists may well first views him as " a masculinist Other" . Thus the studies will be likely to partly misunderstand Lawrence(Ruderman, 249) ; Anne Fernihough in her *D. H. Lawrence*: *Aesthetics and Ideology* (1993) originally argues that his aesthetics "articulate what is essentially the distinction between a pre-Saussurean (mimetic or logocentric) and a post-Saussurean (differential) model of language" (11) ; and in *the Battle of the Sexes in D. H. Lawrence's Prose*, *Poetry and Paintings* (2002) , Cornelis Schulze who even clearly distance herself from feminist criticism, arguing that the symbol of the phallus, much emphasized by Lawrence, has attained " androgynous qualities, not at all involving violence and subordination" as feminists tend to think and appealing readers for allowing "a deeper, a ' whole ' understanding of Lawrence's views on women and his changing presentation of the relationship between the sexes" , which is " an equilibrium in which the battle of the sexes has been transcended" (106 – 115 ; 298 – 296).

Apart from the criticisms above, Morag Shiach studies the theme of work in the novel and affirms the value of physical labour emphasized by Lawrence. She notes that when Mellors insists on his role as productive labourer, Connie's pregnancy and motherhood become her primary occupation. The narrative of her life is created out of affective and domestic relationships. She also mentions other female characters, Hilda and Bolton. About Hilda, she points out that, she "seeks to intervene in her sister's life and is condemned as willful by Mellors in generalizing terms". To Ivy Bolton, she argues that she is "a woman of some determination driven by a clear desire for economic independence" but her nursing training for independence actually leads her to economic, and later emotional, dependency on the Chatterleys(87 – 101).

These female criticisms also more focus on the theme and the protagonists in the novel. Among them, the subversive remarks even appear in the 21st century.

2. 2　Domestic Studies

Compared with the western countries, Chinese are more conservative and traditional on sex. However, in 1936, Lin Yutang translated the French version of the novel into Chinese and praised it as a good book, a healthy book, suggesting readers with a pure heart to read (3 – 5). Yu Dafu also expressed the same praise. Later long-termed wars and the Cultural Revolution in china mostly disrupt the criticism of the novel. Meanwhile, since the People's Republic of China was established, the Chinese version of *LCL*, as a pornographic book, had been forbidden. Until the end of 20th century, the Chinese version of the novel has been accepted legally. However, the English edition of the novel has never been forbidden in China (Miao 77). So the study on the novel has been still a hot subject but its criticisms are far later than the international review in time.

About his philosophy and ideas, until 1998, Wu Houkai introduces them in detail in his book. Later, with the rising interest on the novel, many criticisms start using Lawrence's ideas or philosophy in interpreting it, like Zheng Dahua (2001), Gao Wanlong (2009), and Zhao Cuihua (2007); while some criticisms borrow the review of western feminism, such as Ge Lunhong(2001) who argues that Connie is not a modern woman but an ideal woman in primitive sex who gives up her will set by the author (41 - 44); to the point, Liu Hui(2007) has the similar idea; besides, she attacks Lawrence's patriarchal idea on Bertha (33 - 37); and Wang Yunqiu's (2007) idea is original, who employs "Differance" of Derrida and the view of feminism to pay a tribute to Bertha Coutts, Mellors' wife, arguing that though deprived of the rights of "presence" in the novel, she has strong female self-consciousness. She dares to refuse Mellors and challenge the authority of male. Her "lack" deconstructs the author's hypocritical "tenderness of touch" between Connie and Mellors. She advocates that Connie is figured as a distorted female by the virile author, so the relationship between man and woman the author seeks and argues is a false harmonious balance (135 - 137).

Besides, Pei Yang (1989) further points out that the author's idea is wrong and "man and society" is the most important force to develop but not " man and self". Meanwhile, he praises the narration about nature, sex and symbolic writing in the novel (22 - 27). Miao Fuguang(2007), from the view of ecology, studies the ecological philosophy of the novel: back to nature and argues that the theme is very important and valuable for human being's rethinking the relationship with nature(77 - 80).

2.3　Summary

Being the most controversial novel in Lawrence's works, *LCL* has been attracting a lot of interests in the worldwide for nearly 90 years old. Its charms lie in evoking readers various forms of emotional repulsions. Through the different criticisms above, whether for or against, criticisms on the novel gradually tend towards broader judgments, especially international criticism. For male critics, under the influence of feminism, some have noticed the problems of Lawrence's patriarchal ideas and their own. Thus the criticism for Lawrence moves from extreme support and blind worship into objective and reasonable amendments. For female critics, after Millett, some of them have also changed attitudes, from attacking at the start into wholly and comprehensively understanding and appreciating his work. However it does not mean the review of feminism on the novel can be subverted thoroughly, for the fact that Lawrence's patriarchal ideas existing in his writing can not be ignored and his understanding on gender roles is based on patriarchal metaphysics of presence. Thus, we read Lawrence not only with his philosophy and works together but also keeping distance from his philosophy. To the point, Beauvoir's criticism on Lawrence is more reasonable and objective compared with other female critics, like Anais Nin, Anne Porter, Edith Sitwell, Kate Millett, Simpson and Cornelis Schulze. Her view will be very helpful to support the thesis of the book.

Through the criticisms above, most critics still more focused on the protagonists—Clifford, Connie and Mellors, their triangular relationship and their symbolic meanings. Many of them have commonly moved from Connie's "sexual regeneration" and "spiritual regeneration" to her "passivity in sexuality" and "abandoned female will", while the other female characters, Bertha, Mrs. Bolton, Connie's mother and Hilda, have been far less analyzed yet. The review on Bertha is only mentioned in analyzing Mellors' sexuality or Lawrence's sexual fantasy; Mrs. Bolton is only related to Sir Chatterley's final "male hysteria" (*LCL* 218); and Connie's mother and Hilda are almost neglected. Studies on all women in Lawrence's *LCL* obviously have not been enough and the problem on gender equality also has not been discussed further. Employing the concepts of Beauvoir's "woman as Other for and by men" and Spender's "patriarchal order" in language, the book will analyze the gender roles of the five women in the novel together in order to discuss Lawrence's view on gender equality more comprehensively.

Chapter Three Introduction to Theories

The chapter will present the theoretical framework of my study. Simone de Beauvoir's "woman as Other for men and by men" in *The Second Sex* and Dale Spender's "Patriarchal Order" in *Man Made Language* which will provide the foundation of the analysis on identities or gender roles of the five female characters and gender equality of the novel.

3. 1 Beauvoir's "Woman as Other for and by Men"

The male writer, Benda, states, "Man can think of himself without woman. She cannot think of herself without man". To his saying, Beauvoir explains clearly, "He is the Subject, he is the Absolute—she is the Other" (16). What is woman? In male eyes, woman is "a womb", "a uterus", "the negative", "the imperfect man", "an incidental being" or even "a supernumerary bone of Adam" (15 – 16) while in female and male eyes, man stands for power, law, authority, the positive, superiority or even human beings. The two sexes are obviously unequal.

Otherness is a fundamental category of human being. "The Other is posed as such by the One in defining himself as the One" (Beauvoir 18). However, the Self and the Other were not originally attached to the division of the sexes and not dependent upon any empirical facts. Then why woman as Other and are taught to be woman, remain woman, become woman? Once woman wants to change a little, woman is told that femininity is in danger by man and even woman. Why is she often very well pleased with her role as the Other and complicity?

Beauvoir looks for the answers in biology, psychoanalysis of Freud and Historical Materialism of Engels and the history of woman. She finds out, in biology, the male and the female are not attached to the division of superior and inferior. "Woman, like man, is her body; but her body is something other than herself" (61). When she subordinates to the species, he is free and "maintains his individuality within himself" (55). That's the difference in body but not in mind. In the psychoanalytic point of view, she discovers, psychoanalysts can not explain the origin of "determinism" and "collective unconscious", thus girls are deprived of the idea of choice but only play the symbolic female. As her famous statement claims, "One is not born, but rather becomes, a woman" (295). She explains further that woman's awareness of herself is not defined exclusively by her sexuality. It reflects a situation that depends upon the economic organization of society. In Engels' *The Origin of the Family, Private Property, and the State*, Engels argues that "private property appears: master of slaves and of earth, man becomes the proprietor also of woman. This was 'the great historical defeat of the feminine sex'" (84 – 85). Though Beauvoir questions how it happened Engels'

did not answer, she affirms the historical reality along with the view of exis-
tentialism. As she finds out in biology, female grasp upon the world is less
extended than man's, and she is more closely enslaved to the species (66).
Thus when man gets the dominating position in economic, economic oppression gives rise to the social oppression to which woman is subjected. "[S]-
he is for man as a sexual partner, a reproducer, an erotic object—an Other
through whom he seeks himself" (90). At the moment, even if woman is
oppressed, she does not lose her subjectivity. She is only seen as an Other
for men.

When " [t]he value of muscular strength, of the phallus, of the tool
can be defined only in a world of values; it is determined by the basic pro-
ject through which the existent seeks transcendence" (91), a world in
which males dominate appears. In the world, man always wants to master
and conquer woman but her subjectivity threats male domination. To repress
or extinguish female subjectivity, man in his activity creates his values as
the value of existence (295). "Woman, has come to stand for Nature, Mystery, the non-human; what she represents is more important than what she
is, what she herself experiences" (295 – 679). Real women should not exist in the eyes of men, "but rather a becoming", that is to say, "her *possibilities* should be defined" (66). When woman does not question her "possibilities" but accepts them, being the Other, "towards complicity", she
will help man actualize his deep-seated expectation (21). At this time, she
has lost her subjectivity and unconsciously accepted to be seen as the Other
by men.

Except the women in reality, woman as other by men and for men can
be found out more in literature. Beauvoir argues that male creates female

myth, which often confuses us as if woman is not the other.

> When he describes woman, each writer discloses his general ethics and the
> special idea has of himself; and in her he often betray also the gap between
> this world view and his egotistical dreams (282).

In male language, woman " as the other still plays a role to the extent
that, if only to transcend himself, each man still needs to learn more fully
what he is" (282). Thus, the other women figured by man just serves as
male's transcendence. She is always the object, while he is always the subject. Through her, the hero or the author transcends himself.

In reality, however, if the behavior of flesh-and-blood women is contradicted by the definition of Femininity, it is the woman who is wrong. She is
always seen as Other for man and even for those women who have become
the Other by man unconsciously. As Beauvoir points out, "we are told not
that Femininity is a false entity, but that the women concerned are not feminine" (282 – 283).

Whether woman as the Other for men or by men, her gender role must
be decided by femininity defined by the culture man dominates. Here Beauvoir questions clearly the qualities of femininity and masculinity. In fact,
gender roles are decided by the culture but not by biological sexes. Kate
Millett, drawing upon some brief remarks made by Beauvoir, points out
clearly, the target roles which are defined by patriarchy for the two sexes is
not being " male" or " female" because they are biological terms while
"masculine" and "feminine" are terms defining gender and the roles as-
cribed for each sex (26). Thus Beauvoir suggests, to emancipate woman is
to refuse to confine her to the relations she bears to man, not to deny them
to her; let her have her independent existence and she will continue none

the less to exist for him also— "mutually recognizing each other as sub-ject, each will yet remain for the other an other". That is, through their nat-ural differentiation men and women unequivocally affirm their "brother-hood" (740 – 741).

All in all, being "the Bible of feminism" (Elizabeth 108), *The Second Sex* lies in exploring the root of woman's problems— "male primary and fe-male otherness deadlocked in every human's consciousness" (Felstiner 248). She is seen by and for men, always the object and never the subject (Walter 98). Lawrence, as a male writer with obviously patriarchal ideas, always used his pen to figure and narrate women. According to Beauvoir's "woman as Other", we can find out that there are also two kinds of Other in *LCL*: one is figured as Other for Lawrence and the other is figured as Other by him. They can support my thesis to explore his view on gender e-quality, but Beauvoir's theory does not sufficiently understand the subver-sive power of the imagination in fiction. Spender's view will help my thesis strengthen the point.

3. 2 Spender's "Patriarchal Order"

Man Made Language(1980) is one of the most widely held works by Dale Spender (1943—). It has been valued as "one of the great classics of the women's movement" and " a cornerstone of modern feminist thought" (worldcat,2012). In the book, the author argues that women have been aware that male superiority is a myth. However, male superiority is not be confused with male power, for myth can be exposed and eradicated by knowledge, by a change in consciousness. Although they are different, they are also closely linked, "for male superiority has served as a justification for male power" (5). It is because males have power to be in position to construct the myth of male superiority and to have it accepted; because they have had power to be able to 'arrange' the evidence so that it can be seen to substantiate the myth. Spender argues clearly that 'arrange' the evidence to keep man's myth is language.

As we know, language is our means of classifying and ordering the world: our means of manipulating reality. However, man makes use of language to create a symbolic order of the male-as-norm, "a patriarchal order" (7 − 8). It is in such symbolic order where we are born and when we become members of society and begin to enter the meanings which the symbols represent, we also begin to structure the world so that those symbols are seen to be available. In the symbolic order, we are required to classify the world on the premise that "the standard or normal human being is a male one and when there is but *one* standard, then those who are not of it are allocated to a category of deviation" (8). The standard divides "humanity not into two equal parts but into those who are plus male and those who are minus male" (8). The status of the female is only derived from the status of the male, that is, as Other. It is dangerous that "we enter into the meaning of patriarchal order and we then help to give it substance, we help it to come true" (9).

Spender points out, man and woman are indeed divided on the basis of genitalia; we do construct only *two* sexes; we do insist upon a whole range of gender determined behaviors. We are in "a sex-class system" but only see the construction of *patriarchal order*, " patriarchy everywhere " (9). That is not fair! Spender advocates polarizing female/ male, which should lead to a reasonable conclusion: two sexes should be equal. To actualize the conclusion, "the crux of our difficulties lies in being able to identify and transform the rules which govern our behavior and which bring patriarchal order into existence" (8). She warns us we must use language as our tool but in turn its use structures a patriarchal order because in language there are many linguistic means by which patriarchy has been created. So to construct sexual equality not within a patriarchal order, she suggests that " [e] very aspect of the language from its structure to the conditions of its use must be scrutinized if we are to detect both the blatant and the subtle means by which the edifice of male supremacy has been assembled" (8 –9).

All in all, as Spender's book shows, "Man made language", we should be very careful to recognize the traps of language by man, different patriarchal orders and insist on our aim—equality. Lawrence, being a genius male writer, masters language. His philosophy and works are still pursuing the significance of male as the introduction analyzes. In his language, his representations on male and female obviously promote the myth of male superiority.

Combined with Beauvoir's "woman as Other for and by men", women in *LCL* are powerful examples of Other in Lawrence's patriarchal order.

Chapter Four Women in the LCL

Novels, as a strong weapon of ideology, own "the subversive power of the imagination" (Seldon 132). Being a male writer, Lawrence understands the point. He believes that art is more effective on human soul when compared to abstract philosophy. He argues in *Phoenix*:

> Novels dramatize philosophies and people identify themselves with the characters in the novels as they do with the characters in film (520).

Feminists have also realized the power of literature or language. Beauvoir in *the Second Sex* points out, male creates female myth in literature, which often confuses us as if woman is not the other (280). Spender argues more clearly that patriarchal order in language continues the myth of male superiority, which will destroy to actualize the equality between man and woman (5 – 10). Thus we can not ignore the subversive power of ideology our language and literary works own. After understanding Lawrence's works with his philosophy and experiences, using the feminist perspective to reinterpret his works is necessary.

In studying the novel, some questions are raised to be the focuses as the following: The themes of tenderness and love can overweigh than wor-

ship of phallus? Does Lawrence really write for women as he and other critics say? And what's his view on gender equality? Based on his philosophy,
background and late essays, this chapter will employ the concepts of
"woman as Other for men and by men" by Beauvoir and "patriarchal order" in language by Spender to analyze the gender roles of the five women
in the novel with the findings of Lawrence's gender equality.

4.1　Women as Other for Men in Lawrence's Patriarchal Order

In Lawrence's philosophy, he emphasizes the Father in female principle. Daleski points out, the Father by Lawrence is that manifestation of God
which personifies female values (10). For him, as long as the female accepts the Father, their ideas and behaviors will be "in unconscious faith"
to men. The principle has constituted the sufficient proof that his gender
roles are based on "patriarchal metaphysics of presence" (Akgun 21).
Even in his last period, he still insists on this principle.

For Lawrence, dauntlessness and demureness are the two kinds of femininity, which go two kinds of confidence: cocksure and hensure. He argues
that cocksure women are uneasy but hensure women easy, because hensure
women only have "laid an egg" but not have "a vote", "an empty ink-bottle" or "some other absolutely unhatchable object" (LEA 126 – 127).

In the novel, it is easy to find out the two types of women. Connie's

mother, Hilda and Berths belong to "cocksure women", having strong female who will against men separately in three aspects of society, spirit and
sexuality. They are seen as Other for men in Lawrence's patriarchal order,
for they disobey the femininity praised by their husbands and the author.

4.1.1　Connie's Mother— A "Cocksure Woman" as Other for Men in Society

In Chapter One, Connie's mother is narrated dead. There is very little
information about her in the novel but that's enough to show the author's attitude on the type of women. We know that Connie's mother "had been one
of the cultivated Fabians in the palmy, rather pre-Raphaelite days" (*LCL*
2). Then, what's Fabian? And what does "pre-Raphaelite" mean? The two
words can tell us more information on Connie's mother.

4.1.1.1　Fabian Society

The Fabian Society is not only Britain's oldest socialist society but also
the oldest socialist society in the world (Cole 245). According to the information from the Fabian website, it was one of the original founders of the
Labour Party and is constitutionally affiliated to the party. Since 1884 it has
played a central role in developing political ideas and public policy on the
left. It aims to promote: greater equality of power, wealth and opportunity;
the value of collective action and public service; an accountable, tolerant
and active democracy; citizenship, liberty and human rights; sustainable development; and multilateral international cooperation. Today it counts over
200 parliamentarians in its number. From its beginning the Fabian Society
has offered a forum for women to discuss and debate the issues of the
day. Fabian women, in 1908 formed their own group, who were at the fore-

front of the arguments for gender equality before women won the vote ("*Fabians*" 2012).

It is obvious that Connie's mother as a Fabian, a socialist, will pay much attention to gender equality which is disgusted by men in that patriarchal world.

4. 1. 1. 2　Pre-Raphaelite

The Pre-Raphaelites known as the Pre-Raphaelite Brotherhood which was a group of English painters, poets, and critics, founded in 1848 by William Holman Hunt, John Everett Millais and Dante Gebriel Rossetti. The group's intention was to reform art by rejecting what they considered to be the mechanistic approach first adopted by the Mannerist artists who succeeded Raphaetl and Michelangelo. Hence the name: Pre-Raphaelite. Influenced by Romanticism, they thought that freedom and responsibility were inseparable ("*Pre-Rahaelite*" 2012).

Here, Lawrence used the term of painting to satirize those women who only love spiritual freedom and struggle for it but neglect body's freedom or sex.

4. 1. 1. 3　Connie's Mother—a Quasi-Feminist as Other for Men in Lawrence's Patriarchal Order

During Lawrence's early period of portraying women, he created the type of "new woman" who he called the "dreaming", "spiritual" or "Pre-Raphaelite" woman. These women are spiritually, but not sexually, liberated (Simpson 60). Simpson claims, the "Pre-Raphaelite woman" is a type of feminist (Riedell 331).

Here, the two proper nouns, "Fabian" and "pre-Raphaelite" can prove Connie's mother is a quasi-feminist. The usage of the two words implies that she is an active female socialist. Female socialists first took part in class struggle but "once inside the class struggle, women understood that the class struggle did not eliminate the sex struggle" (Beauvoir 1976's interview). As a socialist, Connie's mother may well know the point that freedom or female freedom is what she wants to pursue and struggle for, even in that last few months of her life.

> she wanted her girls to be "free", and to "fulfill" themselves. She herself had never been able to be altogether herself: it had been denied her. Heaven knows why, for she was a woman who had her own income and her own way. She blamed her husband. But as a matter of fact, it was some old impression of authority on her own mind or soul that she could not get rid of. It had nothing to do with Sir Malcolm, who left his nervously hostile, high-spirited wife to rule her own roost, while he went his own way (*LCL* 3).

Obviously, Connie's mother is an independent and intelligent woman with strong self-consciousness. What she cares mostly is freedom of women. And from the above passage, she is not satisfied with her life. She and her husband seem unlike a couple: the husband behaves indifferent to the wife. They are more like strangers in the same room and do their things by themselves. She realizes the problem between them and blames her husband but he does not care.

Soon after she died, her husband "got a second wife in Scotland, younger than himself and richer. And he had as many holidays away from her as possible: just as with his first wife" (*LCL* 190). "Sir Malcolm was always uneasy going back to his wife. It was habit carried over from the first wife" (*LCL* 204). These words imply Malcolm does not like going home and face his wives or exactly, he wants to escape them. Does not he love them or only the first wife? In the Chapter 18, the idea shows obviously from "Connie was his favorite daughter, he had always liked the female in her. Not so much of her mother in her as in Hilda" (*LCL* 205). Hilda, like the mother, also has strong self-consciousness. The kind of female consciousness blocks love from the man for both of them. It can be sure that he dislikes the quality in woman, the strongly female self-consciousness or female subjectivity in his first wife and first daughter.

Through the narration, Lawrence is more inclined to hint that the woman who pursues freedom cannot have a happy marriage or a good destiny. That is proved by Spender that in patriarchal order, there is only plus male and minus male (7 – 8). Even if independent women such as a female socialist, also feel frustrated in marriage for we can see and feel "patriarchy everywhere" (7), especially at home.

Connie's mother is a "cocksure women" in terms of Lawrence's division, who is also seen as Other for men in his patriarchal order. For him, only being a good wife in family, which is the most important for a woman. Lawrence said ironically, "they (cocksure women) find, so often, that instead of having laid an egg, they have laid a vote, or an empty ink-bottle, or some absolutely unhatchable object, which means nothing to them" (*LEA* 127). In *Men Must Work and Women as Well* (1929), he suggests men need physical labour and women as well. Women's physical labour includes "house-work, house-keeping, rearing children and keep a home going" (*LEA* 281). To women's pursuing broader social identities than before, in *Master In His Own House* (1928), he claims that the "intrusion" of women in men's world can be decided by men's indifferences or "charity". "Men leave the field to women, when men become inwardly indifferent to the field. What women take over is really an abandoned battle" (*LEA* 100 – 101).

For Lawrence, the women who pursue the equal identity in society, just like Connic's mother, are seen as Other for man. In his patriarchal order, men are still the One and Subject in society. Even if Connie's mother owns her social identity—a socialist who can talk about politics freely and take part in the social reforms—that's only because of "men's charity" but not woman's legal right.

In the novel, Lawrence's attack against feminists' suffrage or vote is not obvious in Connie's mother but he blames the failure of marriage all on her, which is enough to uncover his attitude. "She blamed her husband. But as a matter of fact, it was some old impression of authority on her own mind or soul that she could not get rid of " (*LCL* 3). A woman, who wants freedom and is eager to get it but can not in her society and family, may well feel herself so powerless and helpless to change her situation. She feels repressed but as her husband, Sir Malcolm does not want to understand her but choose to escape her. "It had nothing to do with Sir Malcolm, who left his nervously hostile, high-spirited wife to rule her own roost, while he went his own way "(*LCL* 3). Sir Malcolm is innocent. Connie's mother must be responsible for her husband going "his own way", because she is "nervously hostile" and "high-spirited". Escaping her seems to be his only but right way.

However, in Chapter 18, what Sir Malcolm said to Mellors proves what he needs. "I never went back on a good bit of fucking, myself. Though her mother, oh, holy saints!" (*LCL* 213) He needs sex but his wife who is a "pre-Raphaelite" and Fabian woman, pursues spiritual freedom without sexual liberation. This is the main cause why he wants to escape her.

These propose one standard, a male-dominated standard, a Lawrencean standard. They construct a symbolic order of the male-as-norm, a patriarchal order. In the patriarchal order, Sir Malcolm's indifference to his wife is reasonable and all is the wife's fault. Thus in "the last few months of her life", she wanted her daughters to be "free" and to "fulfill themselves" (*LCL* 3). As Beauvoir points out, when being a wife she is not a complete individual, she becomes such a mother: the child is her happiness and her justification. Through the child she is supposed to find self-realization sexually and socially (501). Her two daughters are indeed free. They come back to the university, studying, discussing, dating and trying sex. However, the war comes with the pity of their mother's death.

She died because of "nervous invalid" (*LCL* 3). In fact, according to Hilda, her "[m]other died of cancer, brought on by fretting" (*LCL* 56). Thus Hilda warns Clifford not to run any risks and must carry Connie to see a doctor, who is getting thinner and depressed in marriage. Ironically, Connie's depression is related to her life offered by her lamed husband for she is the ideal woman figured by Lawrence, but Connie's mother in depression must be responsible for her marriage and death alone only because she is a "cocksure woman", a "pre-Raphaelite" and Fabian woman.

Here, the mother is seen as an Other for her husband and the narrator. Her social identity and her subjectivity are disliked and unaccepted by men in Lawrence's patriarchal order.

4.1.2 Hilda—A "Cocksure Woman" as Other for Men in Spirit

Being a socialist, Hilda pursues the same social identity like her mother. She is "always on the side of the working classes" (*LCL* 180). However, the author does not focus on the point but on her will. In Chapter One, Hilda married. Her husband was "a man ten years older than herself, an elder member of the same Cambridge group, a man with a fair amount of money, and a comfortable family job in the government: he also wrote philosophical essays" (*LCL* 4). Hilda's marriage is not happy, too. In Chapter16, "her husband was now divorcing her" (*LCL* 177). Why? Because her appearance is "demure and maidenly as ever" but "she had the same will of her own. She had the very hell of a will of her own, as her husband had found out" (*LCL* 177). Is it her will that destroys her marriage? Yes, Lawrence directly sentences Hilda to the wrongdoer in marriage as he does for Hilda's mother, another "cocksure woman" in spirit defined as by Lawrence.

In the eyes of her father, Hilda is like her mother. As the former mentions, "Connie was his favorite daughter, he had always liked the female in her. Not so much of her mother in her as in Hilda" (*LCL* 205). In the eyes of her husband and the narrator, she has "the very hell of a will of her own" (*LCL* 177); In the eyes of Clifford, she is "a decidedly intelligent woman and would make a man a first-rate helpmate, if he were going in for politics for example" (*LCL* 179). And compared to Connie, she has "none of Connie's silliness, Connie was more a child: you had to make excuses for her, because she was not altogether dependable" (*LCL* 179). In the eyes of Mellors, Hilda is a "stubborn woman an er own self-will" (*LCL* 184). He even criticizes her bitterly for her divorce, "you deserve what you get: to be left severely alone " (*LCL* 184).

Those men's judgments are almost the same view—Hilda has her own will. She is also a "cocksure woman" and disliked by men in that order. Clifford's comment seems less hostile but for him, Hilda's wisdom is only helpful for her husband if he were going in for politics. In patriarchal world, wife is always a helper of her husband even if she has the ability to do it alone. Obviously, a woman pursuing her social identity like a man is not accepted in Lawrence's patriarchal order. She is only seen as an Other for men. Except it, her strong will is a bad thing! Lawrence argues that cocksure women are uneasy but hensure women easy, because hensure women have "laid an egg" but not "a vote", "an empty ink-bottle" or "some other absolutely unhatchable object" (*LEA* 126 – 127). Hilda's dauntless will is not what men expect women have. They dislike her for she has no "demureness" men like. Even in the eyes of Connie, she has the similar idea. "you're too conscious of yourself all the time, with everybody"(*LCL* 190) but Hilda answered, "I haven't a slave nature... At least, I'm not a slave to somebody else's idea of me, and the somebody else a servant of my husband's" (*LCL* 190).

Like her mother, Hilda is such a confident and independent woman too, not willing to be "complicity", "the Other" or "the Object" in the patriarchal society. She is also attacked and rejected by men in Lawrence's patriarchal order for she disobeys the symbolic order of " the male-as-norm" (Spender 6). As Beauvoir points out, " woman has always been man's dependant, if not his slave; the two sexes have never shared the world in equality"(20). So, Hilda's ability in social identity is refused or neglected not only by the male characters but also by the narrator in the novel. Through the description of Hilda, the novel continues to keep the smell of patriarchal ideas, which is more obvious to show Lawrence's attitude to gender equality—he still refuses to accept female subjectivity and social identity equally.

4. 1. 3　Bertha Coutts— A "Cocksure Woman" as Other for Men in Sexuality

Bertha Coutts is Mellors' wife, who never appears in the novel but exists in the narration of other characters (Clifford, Mrs. Bolton and Mellors) and the narrator. According to Clifford, she "went off with ⋯with various men⋯ but finally with a collier at Stacks Gate, and I believe she's living there still" (*LCL* 34). The first impression of readers on Bertha is a slut, unfaithful to her husband. In Chapter 10, Mrs. Bolton strengthens the impression. Mellors is a "nice lad", "quite the gentleman" but he married Bertha Coutts, "as if to spite himself" (*LCL* 106). The following words seem to be said by Mrs. Bolton but also the narrator. "Some people do marry to spite themselves, because they're disappointed of something. And no wonder it had been a failure" (*LCL* 106).

Bolton's "disappointed of something" makes the excuse of the failure of Mellors' marriage and at the same time, the wrong side is tactfully set in Bertha. She is not fit for "nice" Mellors. When Bolton knows Lady Chatterley's lover is Mellors, she claims, "He's the one man I never thought of; and the one man I might have thought of" (*LCL* 107). She does not look at the thing from the perspective of Bertha but from the man's side. She takes part in male "complicity" (Beauvior 21), narrating Bertha according to the male rules. As Spender says, in the symbolic order of language, "we enter into the meaning of patriarchal order and we then help to give it substance, we help it to come true. "(8) So does Mrs. Bolton here.

For Mellors, as Ms. Bolton says, he marries Bertha for he "disappointed of something" (*LCL* 148). In Chapter 14, he confessed his sexual experiences to Connie. The first girl was a school-master's daughter, "pretty, beautiful really" (*LCL* 149) but she egged him on to poetry and reading. She never wanted sex. He left her. The second girl is a teacher. Though she had made a scandal by carrying on with a married man and driving him nearly out of his mind, she loved everything about love, except the sex. He forced her to it, and she could simply numb him with hate. He also left her. He claimed, "I wanted a woman who wanted me, and wanted it" (*LCL* 149). Then he met his neighbor, Bertha Coutts who is "common". He was glad she was common and wanted to be common. The word, "common" uses the meaning of its old-fashioned, an offensive word for someone from a lower social class. Lawrence repeats using the word to describe Bertha in order to make readers believe Bertha is rude, low and obscene while Mellors is different, only spitting himself.

And then Mrs. Bolton continues strengthening the impression further: Bertha, who is "more common than ever", is a liar; "the low, beastly things he did to her" is not unbelievable (*LCL* 198). Clifford's final words are very interesting. He shocked what Bertha said but thought that "unusual sexual positions" with "the Italian way" or "touch of Rablais" was Bertha Coutts herself who "first put him (Mellors) up to them" (*LCL* 201). This kind of understanding, on the contrary, proves that it is not Bertha who can think out these sexual positions but Mellors' "many tricks" (*LCL* 201) or his fantasies on sex.

After all, their marriage is terrible. According to Mellors' narration, he is glad that he can "fuck her like a good un" so he brings her breakfast in bed (*LCL* 149). However, she is not a good wife. She does not get him a proper dinner when he comes home for work, and if he says anything, she throws something like a cup at him. Then they start to fight against each other. However, for Mellors, what's worse, she is not a good lover in bed.

> But when I had her, she'd never come off when I did. Never! She'd just wait. ···And when I'd come and really finished, then she'd start on her own count, and I had to stop inside her till she brought herself off wriggling and shouting, she'd clutch with herself down there, an' then she'd come off, fair in ecstasy. And then she'd say: That was lovely! Gradually I got sick of it: and she got worse... (*LCL* 149).

This scene should be very familiar for Connie, who has to go on after Michaelis has finished and that also enrages him. "I'm darned if hanging on waiting for a woman to go off is much of a game of a man···" (*LCL* 38). Michaelis' words are the crucial blow to her. "It killed something in her" (*LCL* 38). However, when she listens to what Mellors complains like that, she does not defend against him.

In fact, the words from Clifford, Mrs. Bolton and Mellors at the start, indeed make many critics or readers believe that Bertha is in the opposite of the relationship between Connie and Mellors, who are healthy, beautiful and peaceful while Bertha is "obscene" (Moynahan, 105), awful and violent. Here Michaelis and Mellors, as the spokesmen of Lawrence, narrate what they expect women to do in sex: woman should get her pleasure and satisfaction of man at the same time. Is that possible? To female sexuality, Beauvoir argues clearly that,

> Even when a woman overcomes all inner resistance and sooner or later attains the vaginal orgasm, her troubles are not over; for her sexual rhythm and that of the male do not coincide, her approach to the orgasm being as a

rule much slower than the male's (414).

According to the Kinsey Report, generally speaking, three-quarters of males, orgasm is reached within two minutes after the initiation of the sexual relation while women may require ten to fifteen minutes of the most careful stimulation to bring them to climax. If the male is required to match the female partner, he is demanded to be quite abnormal in his ability to prolong sexual activity without ejaculation (qtd. in Beauvoir 414).

For Lawrence, he is so interested in the theme of sex. Why does he make the stupid mistake? Is it his ignorance or his fear? Squires argues, in effect, Lawrence distinguishes clitoral from vaginal orgasm; "it probably has a biographical origin" — he wants to teach his wife how to live with him. Thus he thinks, that Lawrence ignores the scientific date in order to "reform sexuality" appears narrow, only as "his understanding" or "his art" (131). On the point, Torgovnick has the different idea. He points out that, Lawrence has read some works of Havelock Ellis, *Studies in the Psychology of Sex* (1897 – 1928). Thus Lawrence understands female sexuality. The struggles over orgasm between man and woman in *Rainbow* and Mellors' denunciation of Bertha Coutts and of women as lesbians in the novel can not be read simply as part of Lawrence's fear of female sexuality, but the climax of a series of encounter in which man and woman use sex to skirmish with and control each other (42 – 47). However, in his *Studies in Classic American Literature* (1923), Lawrence argues:

> The trouble about man is that he insists on being master of his own fate, and
> he insists on oneness. For instance, having discovered the ecstasy of spiritual
> love, ⋯ He wants his nerves to be set vibrating in the intense and exhilarat-
> ing unison with the nerves of another being, and by this means he acquires an

ecstasy of vision, he finds himself in glowing unison with all the universe (Chapter Six 136).

Unfortunately, Lawrence also knows "this glowing unison is only a temporary thing, because the first law of life is that each organism is isolate in itself, it must return to its own isolation" (136). To make the female partner understand "the ecstasy of spiritual love" of the male in mutual intercourse— the unison with the all universe, Lawrence is trying his best to explore the way of communication. As Beauvoir's analysis shows, it demands that the claims of the ' personality ' are abolished (246). In fact, only female personality is abolished by the author in the novel (Bedient 370). Thus, Bertha's will in sexuality blocks the communication and destroys Mellors' "ecstasy of spiritual love". She is only set up as an anti-case of Connie in Lawrence's patriarchal order, an Other seen for man but not an Other seen by man in sexuality. His aim may be to "reform sexuality" according to his fantasy, by using Squires' phrase.

After narrating that Bertha is not a good wife and lover, the author continues strengthening the failures of her identities. In the end of the story, Bertha comes back to the cottage. She enters the house in the wood with the window broken and lies in bed "without a rag on her" (LCL 197). Mellors offers her money but she wants to be his wife. He leaves but she finds out some evidences: first "a scent-bottle" , "gold-tipped cigarette ends" and then "the initials, C. S. R. " on the back-board of photo frame and one book with Connie's full name, "Constance Stewart Reid" (LCL 97, 2 02). The secret is exposed while Sir Clifford takes legal steps against her. She disappears for she fears the police. Before it, she goes to see her daughter. However, when her daughter sees her, "instead of kissing the loving's mother hand, bit it firmly", she smacks in her face with the other hand which sent the girl reel into the gutter(*LCL* 200). Obviously, she is also not a good mother.

To sum up, Bertha's identities for Mellors, Mrs. Bolton, Connie, and Clifford are failures: she is not a good wife, a good lover or a good mother; she is "common", rude and violent in Lawrence's patriarchal order. For Mellors, she keeps her will ready against him, "always, always: her ghastly female will: her freedom!" (*LCL* 210). Especially what makes him hate her is her will in sexuality for "there's the hard sort, that are the devil to bring off at all, and bring themselves off, like my wife. They want to be the active party"(*LCL* 151). For Mellors, man is the active party while his wife shows as a "cocksure woman" in sexuality, which makes him angry and disgusted.

Wang Yunqiu praises Bertha just like the madwoman in the attic In *Jane Eyre* and argues that she dares to refuse Mellors and challenge the authority of male. Her "lack" deconstructs the author's hypocritical "tenderness of touch" between Connie and Mellors (135 – 137). Her idea is original but Bertha is never the example the feminists praise. As the former analysis, Bertha is only an anti-case of passive Connie set up by the author on purpose. Besides, her "bullying" against Mellors is more related to her background.

Before marring, Bertha goes out to be "a lady's companion" or "a waitress or something in a hotel"(*LCL* 149). Her social experience makes her know what man wants mostly: sensual love, which is the only way she can make use of. Besides, she is from the low class, no education and no status. To knowledge of sexuality, she may well learn more from the gossips of her mother or the wives of colliers. To her behavior, as the author knows, colliers treat their wives often rudely, wildly and carnally, whether in life or in sex. Thus she is likely to mimic the way of his father or other men around her in order to protect herself in that situation. Ironically, Mellors dislikes her but she has "various men" from the low class. If the author wants to prove she is "common", it proves on the contrary that she is normal in her class. If the problem does not lie in her, then it is in Mellors.

In fact, Mellors is indeed different from the working class though he is from it, and at the same time he also different from the upper class. He is educated, clever and gentle for Mrs. Bolton; he is narrated as a "natural aristocrat" (Koh); he is like "a God" who knows everything (Beauvoir 254). Thus, he is not so "common" as his wife from the low class.

Tactfully, Lawrence avoids denouncing "common" colliers or the low class but makes Bertha as a substitute in his patriarchal order. In Beauvoir's words, if the behavior of flesh-and-blood women is contradicted by the definition of Femininity, it is the latter who are wrong (283). Even if she mimics the behavior of "minus man" (Spender 7), she is not accepted by those who are faithful in the patriarchal order such as Mellors, Clifford, Connie, Mrs. Bolton and Lawrence, even including her subjectivity in sexual orgasm. She is the Other for men and their complicity in Lawrence's patriarchal order.

4.2 Women as Other by Men in Lawrence's Patriarchal Order

Lawrence's dual philosophy emphasizes "an absolute degree of masculinity" (Daleski 11). His Father principle in female principles can prove the point obviously. In *LCL*, Mrs. Bolton and Connie are faithful to Lawrence's the Father principle, willing to be the absolute Other defined by Lawrence in his patriarchal order. In his order, they become the male's "complicity" and are often very pleased with their role as the Other (Beauvoir 21). However, only Connie is his ideal woman, a real "hensure woman" in his new patriarchal order. Mrs. Bolton is not a "cocksure mother" again but not a "hensure woman". As the former mentions, a "hensure woman" should have laid an egg but not have laid a vote, or an empty inkbottle, or some absolutely unhatchable object, which means nothing to them (*LEA* 127). In the novel, Mrs. Bolton is a nurse. Her social identity is satirized by Lawrence. Her story will prove that even if the fate forces woman to go out of home to support the family, she will be refused because "she is a hen and not a cock, all she has done will turn into pure nothingness to her" (*LEA* 127) in the patriarchal order.

4.2.1 Mrs. Bolton— Not a "Cocksure Mother" but an Absolute Other by Men

As we know, Mrs. Bolton is a very familiar character in Lawrence's novels. Her archetype is his mother, Lydia Beardsall, who was a daughter of an engineer, from a middle-class family and had taught school. Her husband, Lawrence's father was a miner, hot-tempered, unschooled, and robust. He "hated books, hated the sight of anyone reading or writing" while she hated "the thought that any of her sons should be condemned to manual labour. Her sons must have something higher than that" (*Studies in Classic American Literature* , 125). They had little in common. Their marriage is disastrous. Thus, she devoted her love and expectations to her children, especially Lawrence. As the introduction mentions, Lawrence has complicated emotions to his parents. First, he loves and depends on her mother but hates his father. Then, he gradually likes his father and tries to escape the control and influence of his mother, just like his autobiographical novel, *Sons and Lovers.* For him, his mother is still a cocksure woman.

> The woman of my mother's generation was in reaction against the ordinary high-handed, obstinate husband who went off to the pub to enjoy himself, to waste the bit of money that was so precious to the family. The woman feltherself the higher moral being: and justly, as far as economic morality goes. She therefore assumed the major responsibility for the family, and the husband let her. So she proceeded to mould a generation (*Sons and Lovers* 818).

Jessie Chambers, his first girlfriend, also writes in her *A Personal Record*, " Mrs. Lawrence occupied a remarkable position in her family. She ruled by a sort of divine right of motherhood, the priestess rather than the mother. Her prestige was unchallenged, it would have seemed like sacrilege to question her authority. I wondered often what was the secret of her power, and came to the conclusion that it lay in her unassailable belief in her won rightness" (138).

That makes Lawrence love her mother, fear her and also want to escape her, which influences his attitudes on other women. On one hand, he dislikes those possessive women or "cocksure women"; on the other hand, he feels that they are more powerful than men (Frieda 55). His wife, Frieda was the type of his mother, very cocksure but he married her. According to his letters, he needs her difference to arise the quarrels between them, which can help his genius in writing (Gao 67). In his *LCL* and late essays, he denounces "cocksure women" and promotes "hensure women".

Mrs. Bolton's archetype is his mother but she is not a "cocksure mother" again. As the former analyzes, Mrs. Bolton faithful to the patriarchal order has become male "complicity" (Beauvoir 21), an absolute Other by men. First, in the novel, Lawrence beautifies the marriage of Mrs. Bolton and her emotions to her husband. Her husband is a miner but dies "in an explosion down th' pit" at the age of 28 before 23 years (*LCL* 57). She has loved him deeply and kept the love since he died. She often feels that he'd have to come back and lie against her. She says, "so I could feel him with me. That was all I wanted, to feel him there with me, warm" (*LCL* 120). According to her narration, her husband, Ted Bolton, was a man who cared for nothing and nobody until he saw her first baby born. He was shocked and frightened though he never said anything. Since then, her husband did not dare to sex with her freely. "I don't believe he had any right pleasure with me at nights after; he'd never really let himself go" (*LCL* 119). She told him that she did not care but he did not want her to have any more children for her pain in producing the baby "spoilt his pleasure in his bit of married love" (*LCL* 119). Strangely, his sensitiveness and "the touch of him" without pleasure warms her and even makes her feel proud.

But there, when I look at women who's never really been warmed through by a man, well, they seem to me poor doolowls after all, no matter how they may dress up and gad (*LCL* 120 – 121).

Moreover, she had two children and a baby in arms when he died. Her life was very hard but she never complained. The compensation of three hundred pounds was divided into thirty shillings a week, only supporting the family for four years. Later, " she attended classes in ambulance and then the fourth year took a nursing course and got qualified. She was determined to be independent and keep her children" (*LCL* 57). She first stayed at a hospital and then at her husband's company as the parish nursing. About 23 years later, the baby and the daughter were married. The other one was a schoolteacher. Though she pursues her independence in economy after her husband dies, she never doubts the superior myth of man except feeling the oppression from the upper class.

Besides, her emotions on colliers and masters are different from Mrs. Lawrence. She is from the low class and educated after her husband dies. Because of her education and job, she likes the colliers but at the same time she feels very superior to them. "She felt almost upper class; at the same time a resentment against the ruling class smouldered in her" (*LCL* 57). Thus, the upper classes fascinate her, appealing to her peculiar English passion for superiority. She accepts her new job in Wraby but "one could see a grudge against the Chatterleys peep out in her; the grudge against the masters" (*LCL* 57).

When nursing Clifford, she is clever and competent. "She soon knew how to have him in her power" (*LCL* 59) . To the point, she is like Mrs. Lawrence but in her eyes, all men are babies, which is decided by her

61

job not her motherhood. Gradually, Clifford trusts her and depends on her. Even under her influence, he begins to take a new interest in the miners. "In one way, Mrs. Bolton made a man of him, as Connie never did" (*LCL* 77). However, Clifford is not her son but her master and patient. Apart from it, she loves her husband very much and hates the ruling class.

> And she was thinking of her own Ted, so long dead. Yet for her never quite dead. And when she thought of him, the old, old grudge against the world rose up, but especially against the masters, that they had killed him. They had not really killed him. Yet, to her, emotionally, they had (*LCL* 102 – 103).

When she knows the lover of Lady Challerley is Mellors, she "glanced triumphantly at the already sleeping Clifford" (*LCL* 107).

In the last chapter, Connie exposes her secrels to her husband. Clifford is sad, even shocked though he knows earlier the truth in his heart. To "release his self-pity", Mrs. Bolton's duty is to pull him out (*LCL* 218). She began to weep first. Later, he was weeping for the betrayal of Connie. She laid her arm around his shoulder, kissed him and rocked him on her bosom. Finally, he slept like a child. Her way is successful. However, after this, he ordered her to kiss him and touched her breasts and kissed them in exultation, "the exultation of perversity, of being a child when he was man" (*LCL* 219). According to the narration, Mrs. Bolton was both thrilled and ashamed; she both loved and hated it. Ironically, Lawrence uses "child-man" to describe Clifford and "Magna Mater" (Great Mother) to call Mrs. Bolton (*LCL* 219).

To the ending, Daleski, Ronald and Jackson argue that Clifford's "childish perversity" and Mrs. Bolton's careful nursing make them depend on each other in emotions (113;217;266 – 267). Gerald, from the view of Freud, argues that Clifford's touch is from genital, anal and back to oral of a baby step by step, contrasting with Mellors' touch with Connie: "While Mellors' touch anticipates a freshly eroticized world that will refashion the future, Clifford's touch revives an archaic world of sensations that repeats past identifications" (372). The female critic, Morag Shiach claims that she is "a woman of some determination driven by a clear desire for economic independence" but her nursing training for independence actually leads her to economic, and later emotional, dependency on the Chatterleys (96).

The criticisms do not analyze Mrs. Bolton from her perspective. In fact, even if she depends on her master or patient in emotions or in economy, she is a normal and independent person. Why does she accept the abnormally sexual order from an upper-class "child-man" after she shows that she has loved and missed her husband for over 23 years since he died? It is unreasonable. Besides, her children have grown up and have their families and jobs. In economy, her independence unnecessarily forces her to accept the unreasonable demand. Moreover, in her heart, she hates the ruling class, especially the death of her husband makes her in psyche believe that the masters of colliers are the killers of him.

Thus, the final "perverse" relationship cannot be created from the need of Mrs. Bolton but from Clifford or the author. As we know, the close relationship between Lawrence and her mother is still viewed as the real case of Oedipus complex by the public. John E. Stoll points out, Lawrence's early novels, *The White Peacock*, *The Trespasser*, and *Sons and Lovers*, reveals the attempt of the mother surrogate to assimilate the passive male to her. The incestuous desire is "really the measure of the male's assimilation to that mind, of his longing to be reduced to an adjunct of possessive womanhood (the mother, mother surrogate, or predatory woman as Lawrence comes to call her)" (4). Differently, Clifford is not "the passive male" but an active male or "child". The incestuous desire is what he wants is not Mrs. Bolton. For Lawrence, Clifford's fate is also like his own. Frieda's infidelities and his impotence with serious tuberculosis in the mid – 1920s (Torgovnick 35). According to him, his writing was written by "the passing of the impulse" (Huxley 353). He never corrected his works. Thus, the final ambiguous love between Clifford and Mrs. Bolton is very likely to his impulse to his mother but not to Mrs. Bolton.

Here, the plot is so unreasonable for Mrs. Bolton. At the start, she comforts him in her way for her duty. Later, it's not necessary for her to obey the incestuous order and touch from Clifford. The worst result of her refusal is only that she is quit by him, but it is possible for her to find another job.

Obviously, Mrs. Bolton becomes the receiver of the Oedipus complex from Lawrence. She becomes an Absolute Other, an Object by men in Lawrence's patriarchal order; and even becomes not herself at all. Like the following fate of Connie, she is also "the woman who unreservedly accepts being defined as the Other" in the novel (Beauvoir 254). Different from Connie, she is not the ideal "hensure woman" in Lawrence's new patriarchal order.

4. 2. 2　Connie— A "Hensure Woman" as an Absolute Other by Men

Compared to her mother, Hilda and Bertha, Connie is really a hensure woman in the novel. About Mrs. Bolton, she is not a "cocksure mother" yet is not a hensure woman for she pursues the promotion of her class status in her identities. According to the division of Lawrence, hensure women should obey her duty just like a hen, "having laid an egg" and not having "laid a vote, or an empty ink-bottle, or some other absolutely unhatchable object" (*LEA* 127).

Being a hensure woman, Connie is demure all the time in the novel. Lesie Winter, one of the wealthy coal-miners, her husbands' old acquaintance, thinks her "an attractive demure maiden and rather wasted on Clifford" (*LCL* 93). The narrator also points out, "Connie was gifted from nature with this appearance of demure, submissivemaidenliness, and perhaps it was part of nature" (*LCL* 93). In Clifford's world, she is Lady Chatterley, "the hostess men like so much, so modest, yet so attentive" ((*LCL* 87). She plays the woman so much, it is almost "second nature to her" (*LCL* 87). Here, like those psychoanalysts, Lawrence employs "play". She plays her role, being a demure hostess and never disobeys the second nature. The kind of "play" exposes that she accepts to be an Other defined by men.

According to the plot, at the beginning of the novel, she loves the married life her husband offers her until her father tells her what she has is meaningless and she needs a lover. She indeed listens to him and finds a lover, Michaelis. When he denounces her active position in sexual intercourse, she leaves him with a blow in her heart. She feels empty, loneliness and restlessness in her "womb" (*LCL* 12). After seeing Mellors' naked body in his washing, she starts to feel much more depressed and gets thinner. She needs help and writes a letter to Hilda. In fact, she can help herself but strangely, she does not, for she never disobeys or contradicts her husband. Hilda takes her to see the doctor and finds Mrs. Bolton to take care of Clifford. She is free from the control of him. In fact, she can leave him really but she does not.

She walks in the woods and often goes to see the hens Mellors keeps. Facing new life, the chicks, "her own female forlornness" becomes unbearable and she tears (*LCL* 82). Mellors comforts her with the special way of his own— the closest touch of body, sex. She enters the Mellors' world.

In Mellors' world, she only needs to lie down there, he can have sex with her "like an animal" (*LCL* 97). Her submission is obvious at the start. In the first sex, "she lay still, in a kind of sleep, always in a kind of sleep" (*LCL* 84). and in the second sex, "she lay still, without recoil. Even when had finished, she did not rouse herself to get a grip on her own satisfaction, as she had done with Michaelis; she lay still, and the tears slowly filled and ran from her eyes" (*LCL* 91). For her, he is only a "stranger" (*LCL* 92)! Later, she chooses to avoid him. Ironically and dramatically, she meets him when she comes back from Mrs. Flint. In the third sexual scene, she is forced to lie down there under the boughs of the tree by Mellors. Strangely, Connie feels "all her womb was open and soft" and "another self was alive in her, burning molten and soft in her womb and bowels, and with this self she adored him" (*LCL* 97 – 98). Here, facing Mellors' rude treatment, Connie becomes masochistic completely. As Daleski points out, Lawrence wants to show "a man of power": only Mellors is a wild animal, a 'man', where other men are tame dogs (115). However, Connie is like a student, already awakened, feeling his sexuality with passion (Rudikoff 28). After the fourth sex, she sobbed, "I … I can't love you. "

He answered, "Cnna ter? Well, dunna fret! There's no law says as tha's got to" (*LCL* 127). She follows him, gives up "the inward resistance that possessed her" and accepts everything he tells her. For him, he "needed a silent woman folded in his arm," "sleep, only sleep" (105). Connie is what he wants, demure, obedient, passive and restless while she needs a man, needs to be a mother. Those words on maternity such as "womb", "chicks", "life", "Mrs. Flint's bady" and "cradles" in Wragby, are used to imply the point. As Meyers claims, "the maternal is linked to the sexual theme" (123). Obviously, their relationship is not love but the matter of need. To keep the relationship, she is willing to be a slave of his will, even if he does not love her but her body.

For Mellors or Lawrence, in the new world, women and men pursue "anonymity of being" (Bedient 370). Woman means "womb" (*LCL* 12, 46, 63, 88), "cunt" (131) or "Lady Jane" (170) while man means "balls" (145), "phallus" (156) or "John Thomas" (170). Their marriage is based on "John Thomas" penetrating "Lady Jane". As Mellors says in Chapter Fifteen, "This is John Thomas marryin' Lady Jane" when he puts flowers round Connie's breasts, navel and maiden-hair and his penis, navel and man-moustache (170). He does not mean legal marriage. Thus, when their scandal spreads from Bertha, Mellos is very angry, because according to Hilda's suggestion, he must marry Connie "if they want to live together without being persecuted" (215). For Connie, she also never thinks of marrying Mellors. They only want to sex freely in the wood even if they have their own families in the other world.

Superficially, Lawrence creates a new world where Connie gets spiritual regeneration based on her sexual regeneration and where phallus means "androgynous qualities, not at all involving violence and subordination" (Cornelis 106 – 115). In fact, as Beauvoir and Kate Millet point out, this is a phallus world, a world claiming the superior of male (245 – 254; 238 – 257). The meaning of Lawrence's "phallus", as the psychoanalysts use the terms of phallus, includes the two aspects : literally, it is male's penis; symbolically, it is human's animality, the roots of human being. Man stands for human being and himself while woman is defined as the Other (Beauvoir 70, 245 – 249). To this point, many male critics, such as Daleski, Bedient, Rudikoff and Tindall, also find out that Connie is passive and she has lost her female will in Mellors' world(111 – 115; 370; 411 – 413; 356 – 357). Bedient even points out, Connie and Mellors' desire is "not love, not even tenderness, certainly not joy, but organic peace" (370).

About Mellors' tenderness, from the narration of their sexual intercourses, he is often rude, wild, quick, and short, with angry emotions. His tenderness is not obvious. Only until the end, to encourage him for he does not have courage to face their future with tenderness, Connie risks her one-month pregnancy to satisfy his desire, just requiring him, "Be tender to it, and that will be its future"(*LCL* 209). This sex is tender.

> he realized as he went into her that this was the thing he had to do, to come into tender touch, without losing his pride or his dignity or his integrity as a man (*LCL* 209).

After the sex, he summons up the courage to stay with her. To him, "she is my mate", "a woman who is with me, and tender and aware of me" and "she's not a bully, nor a fool" (*LCL* 209). However, facing many problems left them, he becomes angry again, hating Bertha, Clifford, money, machine and the whole world.

It seems difficult for him to calm down to solve the problems except temporary peace in sexual intercourse. Connie's pregnancy and raising the child will have to influence on their sexual life. If every time he needs sex to peace himself, how long will he can wait? He needs sex, needs "Lady Jane" but not the whole Connie. In his last letter, he writes, "John Thomas says good night to Lady Jane" (*LCL* 227) but not Mellors says good night to Connie.

Thus Simpson's "phallus worship" in "love and gentleness" (13) is not reasonable. Phallus worship is obvious, while love and gentleness are ambiguous. Whether in Clifford's world or in Mellors' world, Connie is playing her role the men ask her to do, passive and obedient. Mellor's world is still a patriarchal world, where he makes his language, the dialect she needs to learn and creates his symbolic order, a phallus's order. The order continues keeping the myth of male superiority. It is obvious that the order is still a patriarchal order. As Squires suggests, "Lawrence should have made Connie a more critical listener. To make the program (a new world) artistically valid, he should have made Connie question Mellors' assumptions, prick them with counterstatement as she does Clifford's, and show lively intellectual interest in his solution" (133). In Lawrence's patriarchal order, Connie accepts all Mellors says without hesitation.

Though Mellors' world is only a utopian fantasy, it is a new patriarchal order by Lawrence. In the new patriarchal order, Connie only escapes from the control of a man (Clifford) into another man's (Mellors). For Lawrence, she is his hensure woman in the order, a true woman with femininity a man likes, who can understand the mystery of universe Mellors or the author understands in reaching orgasm simultaneously. That's his aim, the real unison or communication of two poles. To actualize the aim, the heroine is deprived of her clitoral orgasm in sexual intercourse and also must serve the male's will and idea in his patriarchal order. Connie is his myth of woman, "the women who unreservedly accepts being defined as the Other" (Beauvoir254) —she is defined as an absolute Other by Lawrence. She only play her role like a hen, only wanting to be a lover, wife and mother, faithful to Lawrence's patriarchal order— the Father principle.

4.3   Lawrence's Gender Views

Based on the former analysis, Lawrence's views on gender equality still carry the thick colors of patriarchy in his last period. As his philosophy shows, to female identities, man's world is outside, dealing with abstract issues while women only exist as men's sexual mates of the home, "woman for him exists only in the twilight [⋯] Evening and the night are hers" (F 109). To let women stay home obediently, he argues that women must obey the Father principle, that is, the patriarchal symbolic order. Only in that case, women can accept the female values completely and unconsciously the patriarchal order defines. As Daleski points out, for Lawrence, the Father is that manifestation of God which personifies female values (10).

In *LCL*, the female characters— Connie's mother, Hilda and Bertha Coutts, do not obey the female principles. They have strong female will against men. In the author's narration, they are disliked by their husbands, who want to escape them. In marriage, they are failures. Their pursuit of freedom—whether the social identities of well-educated Connie's mother and Hilda or the individual identities of Bertha from the low class— is denounced by Mellors and the narrator in the novel. For Lawrence, they are "cocksure women" and they are "uneasy" unless they become hensure.

> It is all an attitude, ⋯ And when it has collapsed, and she looks at the eggs she has laid, votes, or miles of type-writing, years of business-efficiency, suddenly, because she is a hen and not a cock, all she has done will turn into pure nothingness to her (" *Cocksure Women and Hensure Men*" *LEA* 126)

For him, women should obey their traditional gender roles just like Connie. Though she accepts a good college education and is born in a socialist or quasi-feminist family, she always obeys her duty of "a hen", being an absolute Other in the patriarchal order. She never disobeys the male's will. Her education and intelligence both are used to serve the male. She helps her husband writing and never thinks she can be a writer; she accepts Mellors' everything and never doubts it; she only wants to be a lover, wife and mother and never wants to pursue her other identities in society. She is always passive, obedient, demure and tender. She accepts the patriarchal order of her husband's world. Although in the end she is against him, she's never against the patriarchal order. Thus, she is easy to accept another man's order and never doubts it. This is the effect of Lawrence's Father principle in female values. Such woman never changes, who has become the male's "complicity" (Beauvoir 21). In his article, *Do Women Change* (1929), he argues as follows,

> In fact I am sure there have been lots of women like ours in the past, and if you'd been married to one of them, you wouldn't have fond her any different from your present wife. Women are women. They only have phrase (*LEA* 151).

These phrase include "first the slave: then the obedient helpmeet: then the respected spouse: then the noble matron: then the splendid woman and citizen, then the independent female, then the modern girl…. " (*LEA* 153)

Lawrence appeals to men, "the fact of life is that women *must* play up to man's pattern. And she only gives her best to a man when he gives her a satisfactory pattern to play up to. … if they want to anything from women, let them give women a decent, satisfying idea of womanhood…" (" *Give Her Pattern*" *LEA* 165). His "a decent, satisfying idea of womanhood" is based on love. "Love itself is a flow, … And only the flow matters: live and let live, love and let love" (*LEA* 155). According to him, "No woman does her housework with real joy unless she is in love" ("*Sex Appeal*" *LEA* 148).

What is love? For him, "sex is the central to love" (Priest 58). *LCL* can be said a complete declaration of his sexual theory. In his eyes, sex has rich connotations. First, it is life, is beauty and is fire. It stands for or is passion, warmth and love. Second, it is the closest touch of man and woman, which is also the important ritual that man and woman experience death and rebirth of personality. The ritual of sex can make woman and man reach their balance and their own wholeness. Third, sex is shameless. It is natural instinct. Releasing the instinct, one can be healthy and of vigour and in unison with "the rhythmic cosmos" (Squires 131). Fourth, sex is the future of human beings. However, in the novel, he sets up tactfully the e-quivalence between 'sexual' and 'phallic', stating the supremacy of the male (Beauvoir 248). This phallic world still constructs another patriarchal order, Lawrence's new patriarchal order.

In his new patriarchal order, when a woman becomes the slave of love or sex like Connie, she can play up to the pattern a man wants her to be: only being a lover, wife and mother well. Female gender roles are still based on the needs of men. The novel ends with waiting of the two lovers. Though the author doesn't answer what Connie will do, according to his narration of other female characters, we can know that Connie will do nothing, only staying in the house. In the end of the novel, Connie must spend a period of pregnancy and "motherhood is set to become her primary occupation" (Shiach 101). Besides, she has "twenty thousand pounds in trust" her mother leaves her and she can spend six hundred a year (*LCL* 90, 160), which can lasts about 33 years. It is unnecessary for her to work. For housekeeping, she can employ a maidservant if she is not willing to do. However, Mellors is different. He can not be just her "male concubine" (*LCL* 207). He needs a job, needs to earn money to keep "the viability of their relationship" even if he hates money (Shiach 100 – 101).

Man is the only breadwinner in Lawrence's patriarchal order. "When a man is clutched by his family, his deeper social instincts and intuitions are all thwarted, he becomes a negative thing. Then the woman, perforce, becomes positive, and breaks loose into the world" ("*Matriarchy*" *LEA* 106). Thus, he argues that, even if women want to be the master of the house, like ancient matriarchy, it is nothing fearful, "give them their full independence and full self-responsibility as mothers and heads of the family. When the children take the mother's name, the mother will look after the name all right" ("*Matriarchy*" *LEA* 106). For him, raising children is always women's duty they can not escape.

Mrs. Bolton is a mother in the novel. For her identities, Lawrence's view is a paradox. She is not a cocksure woman but also not a hensure woman. Her husband dies but she does not marry again. In her heart, she always loves him. However, she has three children to support. She takes a nursing course and gets qualified. She does the nursing job in society. She raises her children independently. Her "motherhood" and her faithful love to her husband are praised by the narrator in the novel. However, she takes part in the job of earning money beyond home and wants to promote her class-status. Her ending seems ironic set by the author on purpose. She accepts Clifford's sexual demands actively in his writing but forgets her deep love for her dead husband and deep hatred for the upper class.

From the perspective of Mrs. Bolton, the ending is not reasonable. According to Lawrence's experiences, philosophy and writing impulse, Mrs. Bolton becomes obviously the receiver of the Oedipus complex from him. In his patriarchal order, she becomes an Absolute Other, an Object by men; and even becomes not herself at all. Her fate is tragic compared to Connie. Even if she is faithful to the Father principle, faithful to the patriarchal order; even if she is forced to go out of home to support her three children after her husband dies; her social identity is a mistake in Lawrence's patriarchal order.

In Lawrence's view, female identities or gender roles should be limited to the traditional identities—be lover, wife and mother at home. She can accept college education; can enjoy free love and also can have sexual experiences before marriage; but she must be faithful to the Father principle, faithful to the patriarchal order. Besides, she should be a hen staying at home but not a cock in society. She should be continue to accept to be an absolute Other defined by men but not to be an Other seen for men in his patriarchal order. She should give up her subjectivity submissively and listen to the will and the way of the male in body and spirit.

In the novel, his themes of love and tenderness are overwhelmed by his worship of phallus. He still states the absolute significance of male over female, whose gender equality is based on his patriarchal ideas. In *LCL*, he does not write for woman but for man and for himself. His language still constructs a patriarchal order but not an equally symbolic order of two sexes.

Chapter Five Conclusion

D. H. Lawrence indeed had unconventional personal life and works. His best friend, Middleton J. Murry calls him as "the outlaw of modern English literature" and "the most interesting figure in it" (214). However, though he "rejects Christianity and Platonism" (Dobree 346), mistrust the existing politics and government (Milne 211) and pursues "natural communism" (Wyndham 121), he never questions the patriarchal order. To his own gender roles or identities, though he realizes that he has the female and male elements in him, he aims at building the absolute significance of male and claiming the absolute differences between masculinity and femininity in order to "regain innocence in sex" (Murry 347). His writing is still patriarchal, not representing as "guidebooks for women" as he said (qtd. in Beauvoir 253).

5. 1   Findings of the Study

In *LCL*, Lawrence constructs a high theme on human being's annihilation and regeneration through "mystical sexual religion" (Undset 353) — describes the sexual relation as a war to the death and rebirth between man and woman. Thus, he was regarded as "a highly moral writer" in 1960s (*Twentieth-Century Literary Criticism* volume2 342). That's why many critics and readers, especially male, like him and support him.

Under the good reputation of the high theme, Connie's wholly passivity in sex and abolition of personality have been found out by many critics such as the female critics Beauvoir, Porter and Millett and the male critics Daleski, Squires, Tindall and Rudikoff.

For Lawrence, man and woman, who are like two separate poles, can enjoy the unison with "the rhythmic cosmos" (Squires 130) by sex as long as the female obeys the male's will and way in body and mind. In the novel, Connie is such a woman who can blend herself with Mellors, enjoy the simultaneous orgasm with him and successfully receive the secrets of the universe he wants to communicate in sex— blending with the trees, the light and the rain. That is the "verity of Life", in which "the human being has its roots" (Beauvoir 245 – 246).

Besides, women are free to choose lovers and marry whoever they want, and even can accept college education as men does in the novel. However, these superficial freedom argues by the author is based on the profits of male. According to Murry, Lawrence's doctrine derived from his experience and his experience will conform to his doctrine (347). Like Mellors' sexual experience, the author's first lover was Jessie who loved talking literature with him and feared sex; and then he had a number of unsatisfactory relationships with the schoolteachers who refused to make love with him for another two years and later he met Frieda, who believed that "If only sex were 'free' the world would straightaway turn into a paradise" under the influence of the disciple Freud, Otto Gross(Frieda 3). Those intellectual females made him feel frustrated and shocked in sex but at the same time, he appreciated their intellects because from his letters, Siegel, found out his "intellectually submissive" — he relied on the comments of others, often women, to improve his work (42). Except intellect, he hoped the female accept sexual emancipation for as his experience shows, when he needed sex, he was often refused by the female.

In his eyes, Frieda was the right woman he wanted. She made him shocked and satisfied for she was intellectual and unconventional. Thus, in his novels, the ideal women set up by him are always intellectual, free-love and sexual-experienced. However, Frieda is his wife but not his ideal woman because she also is the type of his mother, very cocksure but he married her. According to his letters, he needs her difference to arise the quarrels between them, which can help his genius in writing (Gao 67). In his private life, there is indeed the physical violence towards Frieda (Priest 58). She also mentions it in her book. In his inner heart, he hates female will against men.

As Beauvoir points out clearly in *Myth and Reality* of her book, in men's eyes, "it is not enough to have a woman's body nor to assume the female function as mistress or mother in order to be a 'true woman'. In sexuality and maternity woman as subject can claim autonomy; but to be a 'true woman' she must accept herself as the Other" (291). So when Connie subordinates her existence to that of Mellors, he "pays her an infinite tenderness and gratitude" (Beauvoir 250). She is his "true woman", a "hensure woman" — an absolute Other seen by men in Lawrence's patriarchal order.

Contrasting with Connie, her mother, her sister and Mellors' wife are masculine women or "cocksure women", who have strong female-will against men. Connie's mother belongs to the type of "cocksure woman" in society, Hilda the type of "cocksure woman" in spirits and Bertha the type of "cocksure woman" in sexuality, who are denounced bitterly by the hero, the narrator or the author. In their eyes, they are not "true women" but the Other for men in Lawrence's patriarchal order.

Mrs. Bolton is different. She is an independent mother, faithful to the patriarchal order. The author's attitude to her is ambiguous and contradictory. On the one hand, her husband dies and she must stand the duty of the breadwinner to raise the left three children, which is what a mother should do; On the other hand, she takes part in the social identity, finding a nursing job. During her pursuing the promotion of class status, the author arranges on purpose for her to accept the "perverse" relationship with her master, Clifford, actively and incestuously as if she forgets her love for husband and hatred for ruling classes. In fact, according to her situation, she can refuse the unreasonable order of Clifford but the author refuses to do like that. Unlike Connie with "twenty thousand pounds in trust" (LCL 90), Mrs. Bolton must earn money to support her children. Ironically, as an absolute Other faithful to Lawrence's patriarchal order, her social identity at the end of novel is satirized by the author, linked to the mistress of Clifford.

Thus, in his utopian world, "true woman" or "hensure woman" should stay home, avoiding become "independent female, instruments, instruments for love, instruments for work, instruments for politics, instruments for pleasure" ("*Do Women Change*" *LEA* 153).

Though he creates his utopian world, a new patriarchal order, where there are no classes, no governments, no politics, no economic relationships, no industrial civilization and nothing else except women and men in nature; even if in such a world, women still obey the will and way of men. His patriarchal ideas are rooted in his mind and language. As Spender exposes, man makes use of language to construct his symbolic order of the man-as-norm, a patriarchal order, in which man has had power to keep or continue the myth of male superiority (5 – 8). In the novel, Connie actively learns Mellors' language, the dialect and accepts all he says, never questioning his idea. Even she goes against her husband with Mellors' idea, she never questions the authority of them, never questions the superiority of men. She, as Lawrence's "myth of woman", unreservedly accepts being defined as the other (Beauvoir 254).

As we know, novels as a strong weapon of ideology, owns "the subversive power of the imagination" (Seldon 132). Thus, after understanding Lawrence's philosophy and works, using the feminist perspective to reinterpret his works is necessary. The female critic, Cornelis Schulze, because of clearly distancing herself from feminist criticism, argues that the symbol of the phallus by Lawrence has attained "androgynous qualities, not at all involving violence and subordination" as feminists tend to think (106 – 115). Obviously, she is cheated by the symbolic meaning of the phallus. Lawrence is one of the first novelists to introduce themes of modern psychology into his fiction. Like those psychoanalysts, his phallus is based on "patriarchal metaphysics of presence" (Akgun 21). His phallus is the mystical power that motivates the union of man and woman and also is the male's penis (Beauvoir 248 – 250). Subtly and tactfully, man stands for the power of human being and himself as an individual, while woman becomes a subordinate of phallus.

All in all, in his patriarchal order, Lawrence advocates, woman should continue to accept to be an Other defined by men, being a "hensure woman" but not to be an Other seen for men, a "cocksure woman". For him, being lover, wife and mother at home are what female gender roles consist of. The Other identities are not what a woman should do. She should be faithful to the Father principle; should be faithful to the patriarchal order, or the roles of two sexes are inverted, neither natural nor healthy for the society (*F* 141).

5.2   Reflections on Gender Equality

Nowadays, women have got the abstract equality in law but in life, there are still many obstacles in practicing female equality (Beauvoir "*The Second Sex* 25 *years later*" the interview). According to a report in 2009 published in *Academe*, gender-based obstacles in social identities, including low salaries, appointments at low ranks, slower rates of promotion and lower rates of retention, and less recognition through awards, have been described extensively (*"So Few Women Leaders"* 25).

Even in the career as teacher with less sex discrimination, there are raising questions about the root cause for persistence of gender inequity at the highest ranks of academic leadership. For example, women in academia often come across the conflicts between biological and career clocks —the timing of tenure decisions often coincides with the optimal childbearing years. Moreover, women academics who have children still shoulder the majority of domestic responsibilities, and those with children of prekindergarten age are less likely to be in a tenure-track job than their male counterparts (*"So Few Women Leaders"* 26 – 27). Even if they overcome these difficulties, they are difficult to cope with the position for it that demands more private time to devote, which their husbands or families often can not accept. Besides, most leaders they need to cooperate with are male, who like male-dominated communication.

Thus, professional females still face double patriarchal stresses from the society and the family in our age. With fiercer competitions on finding jobs, some men even argue that women should be back to home to reduce the stress of employment. We can see, whether in reality or in novels, patriarchal idea still exists around us. Facing obstacles, we should insist on our equal rights. As men have, the right to choose is also in hand of women. Moreover, in the same world, man and woman should understand and respect each other. Both should be build "their brotherhood" through their natural differentiation— mutually recognizing each other as subjects, each will yet remain for the other an other (Beauvoir 740 – 741). As Spender advices, we are in "a sex-class system" which includes polarizing male and female; then male should not be presented as superior and keep a patri-archal order; we should enjoy equals(9).

It is obvious that the problem on gender equality has not been solved yet. We have a long way to struggle for it in reality and language. In fact, as everyone knows, man and woman coexist for each other in the same world. Then that they both need cooperate and build win-win relationship but not conflict argued by Lawrence should be reasonable, feasible and mu-tually beneficial. However how to cooperate and build win-win realtionship is still and will be still a problem for every man and woman to think about, to explore further and work out. It needs you and me to take part in the case, to do it and especially to educate the young generation after genera-tion, making them understand what is gender equality, what are physiologi-cally sexual differences and what men and women should do to enjoy them-selves and improve themselves equally, harmoniously, and mutually in a win-win relationship. Let's make great efforts hand in hand to welcome the coming day!

References

Akgun, Ela. "An Analysis of Gender Issues In The Lost Girl and The Plumed Serpent By D. H. Lawrence". Middle East Technical University, 2005. Web. 7 May. 2012.

Baldick, Chris. "Lawrence's Critical and Cultural legacy". *D. H. Lawrence*. Ed. Aanne Fernihough. Shanghai: Shanghai Foreign Language Education Press & Cambridge University Press, 2003: 253 – 268. Print.

Beauvoir de Simone. *The Second Sex* . Trans. H Parshley. London: Vintage, 1997. Print.

Beauvoir de Simone. "The second sex 25 years later"-the interview with Simone de Beauvoir by John Garassi. Southapton University. 1976. Web. 19 Apr 2012.

Bell, Michael. " Lawrence and Modernism " . *D. H. Lawrence*. Ed. Aanne Fernihough. Shanghai: Shanghai Foreign Language Education Press & Cambridge University Press, 2003. 179. Print.

Bedient, Calvin. "The Radicalism of 'Lady Chatterley's Lover". 1966. *Twentieth-Century Literary Criticism*. Ed. Dedria Bryfonski and Sharon K. Hall. Vol. 2. Gale Research Inc. 1979: 370 – 371. Print.

Craig, Alec. *A History of the Conception of Literary Obscenity*. Cleveland, OH. : World Publishing, 1963. 146. Print.

Cole, Margaret. "The Fabian Society". *The Political Quarterly*: 245 – 256. CashlOnline. Web. 19 Apr 2012.

Cowan C. James. "Lawrence, Joyce, and the Epiphanies of 'Lady Chatterley'sLover'". 1985. *Twentieth-Century Literary Criticism*. Ed. Laurie DiMauro. Vol. 48. Gale Research Inc. 1993: 140 – 145. Print.

Daleski, H. M. "The Duality of Lawrenc". *Modern Fiction Studies* 5. 1 (1959: Spring) :3 – 18. Cashl Online. Web. 19 Apr 2012.

Daleski, H. M. The Forked Flame: A Study of D. H. Lawrence. 1965. Twentieth-Century Literary Criticism. Ed. Laurie Di Mauro. Vol. 48. Gale Research Inc. 1993: 110 – 117. Print.

Draper, Ronald P. "Chapter 6: The Late Novels: The Plumed Serpent and Lady Chatterley's Lover. " *D. H. Lawrence*. Ronald P. Draper. New York: Twayne Publishers, 1964. Twayne's English Authors Series 7. *Literature Resources from Gale*. Web. 8 June 2012.

Dobree, Bonamy. "D. H. Lawrence". *The Lamp and The Lute*. 1929. Twentieth-Century Literary Criticism. Ed. Dedria Bryfonski and Sharon K. Hall. Volume2, Gale Research Inc. 1979: 346. Print.

Eliot, T. S. " Foreword to D. H. Lawrence and Human Existence". 1951. *Twentieth-Century Literary Criticism*. Ed. Dennis Poupard. Vol. 9. Gale Research Inc. 1983: 219 – 220. Print.

Ellis, E. L. "Havelock Ellis". *The Bookman* 47. 5 (July 1918): 558. Gale. Web. 7 Nov 2010.

Elizabeth Wright. Lacan and Postfeminism. Trans. Wang Wenhua. Beijing:

Beijing University Press. 2005. Print.

Frieda. *Not I, But the Wind.* New York: The Viking Press, 1934. Print.

Fernihough, Anne. "Introduction". *D. H. Lawrence.* Shanghai: Shanghai Foreign Language Education Press & Cambridge University Press, 2003. 1 – 11. Print.

Fernihough, Anne. *D. H. Lawrence: Aesthetics and Ideology.* Oxford: Clarendon Press, 1993. Print.

"Fabians". Web. 20 Mar 2002. < http://www. fabians. org. uk/about-the-fabian-society >

Felstiner, M. Lowenthal. "*Seeing The Second Sex Through The Second Wave*". *Feminist Studies* 6. 2 (1980: Summer): 246 – 276. Cashl Online. Web. 19 Apr 2012.

Gregor, Ian. "The Novel as Prophecy: 'Lady Chatterley's Lover'". 1962. *Twentieth-Century Literary Criticism.* Ed. Laurie Di Mauro. Vol. 48. Gale Research Inc. 1993: 95 – 102. Print.

Gerald, Doherty. "The Chatterley/Bolton Affair: The Freudian Path of Regression in Lady Chatterley's Lover". *Language & Literature* 1998: 372 +. Gale. Web. 7 Apri 2010.

Haegert, John. "H. Lawrence and the Ways of Eros". *The D. H. Lawrence Review* 11 (1978): 199 – 233. Cashl Online. Web. 19 Apr 2012.

Jackson, Dennis. "The 'Old Pagan Vision': Myth and Ritual in Lady Chatterley's Lover. " *The D. H. Lawrence Review* 11 (1978): 260 – 271. Cashl Online. Web. 19 Apr 2012.

Kermode, Frank. *Modern Essays.* London: Fontana Press, 1990. 155. Print.

Koh, Jae-Kyung. "D. H. Lawrence's world vision of cultural regeneration in Lady Chatterley's Lover. " *The Midwest Quarterly* 43. 2 (2002): 189

+. Gale. Web. 7 April 2010.

Lawrence, D. H. *Fantasia of the Unconscious and Psychoanalysis and the Unconscious*. Great Britain: Penguin Books, 1971. Print.

Lawrence, D. H. "A Props of ' Lady Chatterley's Lover ' " 1929. *Twentieth-Century Literary Criticism*. Ed. Dennis Poupard. Vol. 9. Gale Research Inc. 1983:217 – 218. Print.

Lawrence, D. H. *Phoenix: The Posthumous Papers of D. H. Lawrence*. Ed. Edward D. Mc Donald. England: Penguin Books, 1985. Print.

Lawrence, D. H. *Sons and Lovers*. New York: Bantam Books, 1985. Print.

Lawrence, D. H. *Studies in classic American literature* . Ed. Seltzer. NewYork : 1923. Online. Ed. Janet Haven. 1998. Web. 21 Apr 2012.

Lawrence, D. H. *Lady Chatterley's Love*r. Beijing: China's External Economic Trade Press, 2000. Print.

Lawrence, D. H. *Late Essays And Articles*. Ed. James T. Boulton. UK: Cambridge University Press, 2004. Print.

Lyon, John M. "Lady Chatterley's Lover: Overview. " *Reference Guide to English Literature*. Ed. D. L. Kirkpatrick. 2nd ed. Chicago: St. James Press, 1991. Gale. Web. 7 Apr 2010.

Leavis, F. R. *D. H. Lawrence: Novelist*. London: 1955. Print.

Millett Kate. *Sexual politics*. London: Virago, 1977. 238 – 257. Print.

Meyers, Jeffrey. *D. H. Lawrence and the Experience of Italy*. 1982. *Twentieth-Century Literary Criticism*. Ed. Laurie DiMauro. Vol. 48. Gale Research Inc. 1993:120 – 123. Print.

Milne, Drew. "Lawrence and Politics of Sexual Politics". *D. H. Lawrence*. Ed. Aanne Fernihough. Shanghai: Shanghai Foreign Language Education Press & Cambridge University Press, 2003:197 – 215. Print.

Miller Henry. *The Henry Miller Reader.* 1959. *Twentieth-Century Literary Criticism.* Ed. Dedria Bryfonski and Sharon K. Hall. Vol. 2. Gale Research Inc. 1979:366. Print.

Murray, Brian. "D(avid) H(erbert Richards) Lawrence". *British Short-Fiction Writers*, 1915 – 1945. Ed. John Headley Rogers. Detroit: Gale Research, 1996. Gale. Web. 19 Apr 2012.

Murry J. Middleton. " a review of ʻLady Chatterley's Loverʼ ". 1929. *Twentieth-Century Literary Criticism.* Ed. Laurie Di Mauro. Vol. 48. Gale Research Inc. 1993: 91 – 93. Print.

Murry J. Middleton. *Son of Woman.* 1931. *Twentieth-Century Literary Criticism.* Ed. Dedria Bryfonski. Vol. 2. Gale Research Inc. 1979:346 – 348. Print.

Murry J. Middleton. "The Nostalgia of D. H. Lawrence", 1921. *Twentieth-Century Literary Criticism.* Ed. Dennis Poupard. Vol. 9. Gale Research Inc. 1983: 214 – 215. Print.

Moore Olive. "Further Reflections on the death of a Porcupine. " *the Apple is Bibbten Again.* London n. d. 161. Web. 7 May 2012.

Moore T. Harry. *The Priest of Love.* London: Heinemann, 1974. 493. Print.

Moi, Toril. "Sexual / Textual Politics. " *Twentieth Century Western Critical Theories.* Ed. Zhu Gang. Shanghai: Shanghai Foreign Language Education Press, 2001. 237. Print.

"Pre-Raphaelite". Wikipedia. 2012. Web. 20Mar2012. < http://en. wikipedia. org/wiki/Pre-Raphaelite >

Popawski Paul. " Guide to further reading". *D. H. Lawrence.* Ed. Aanne Fernihough. Shanghai: Shanghai Foreign Language Education Press & Cambridge University Press, 2003. 271 – 274. Print.

Potter, Stephen. *D. H. Lawrence: A First Study*. London: 1930. Print.

Porter A. Katherine. " A Wreath for the Gamekeeper" . 1960. *Twentieth-Century Literary Criticism*. Ed. Dedria Bryfonski. Vol. 2. Gale Research Inc. 1979: 367. Print.

Priest, A. Marie. "Married sex: Ann-Marie Priest highlights the importance of D. H. Lawrence as a proselytiser for the role of sex in love and marriage. " *Meanjin* 66. 1 (2007): 58 +. Gale. Web. 7 April 2010.

Riedell, Karyn. "Hilary Simpson, D. H. Lawrence and Feminism (Book Review)", *English Literature in Transition* (1880 – 1920), 26: 4 (1983): 331 – 333. Cashl Online. Web. 19 Apr 2012.

Rudikoff, Sonya. "D. H. Lawrence and Our Life Today". *Commentary*, 28 (1959): 408 – 413. Cashl Online. Web. 19 Apr 2012.

Ruderman, Judith. "Lawrence Among the Women: Wavering Boundaries in Women's Literary Traditions. " *Studies in the Novel* 25. 2 (1993): 249 +. Cashl Online. Web. 28 Mar 2012.

Seldon Raman, Winddowson Peter and Brooker Peter. *A Reader's Guide to Contemporary Literary Theory*. Beijing: Foreign Language Teaching and Research Press, 2004. Print.

Sanders, R. Scott. " Lady Chatterley's Loving and the Annihilation Impulse. " 1985. *Twentieth-Century Literary Criticism*. Ed. Laurie Di Mauro. Vol. 48. Gale Research Inc. 1993: 134 – 140. Print.

Squires, Michael. "The Creation of Lady Chaterley's Lover. " 1983. *Twentieth-Century Literary Criticism*. Ed. Laurie Di Mauro. Vol. 48. Gale Research Inc. 1993: 129 – 134. Print.

"So Few Women Leaders". *Academe*. Jul/Aug 2009, Vol. 95. Issue 4: 25 – 27. Cashl Online. Web. 19 Apr 2012.

Showalter Elaine. "A Literature of Their Own". *Twentieth Century Western Critical Theories*. Ed. Zhu Gang. Shanghai：Shanghai Foreign Language Education Press,2001. 241. Print.

Spender Dale. *Man Made Language* . Routledge & Kegan Paul, 1980. Feminist Online. Web. 19 Apr 2012.

Sitwell Edith. *Taken Care of* ：*An Autobiography*. 1965. *Twentieth-Century Literary Criticism*. Ed. Dedria Bryfonski. Vol. 2. Gale Research Inc. 1979；369 – 370. Print.

Schulze Cornelis. *The Battle of the Sexes in D. H. Lawrence's Prose*,*Poetry and Paintings*. Heidelberg：C. Winter, 2002. Cashl Online. Web. 28 Mar 2012.

Shiach Morag. "Work and Selfhood In *Lady Chatterley's Lover*". *D. H. Lawrence*. Ed. Aanne Fernihough. Shanghai：Shanghai Foreign Language Education Press & Cambridge University Press,2003. 87 – 101. Print.

Simpson, Hilary. *D. H. Lawrence and Feminism*. Groom Helm Ltd, 1982. Print.

Stoll E. John. *The Novels of D. H. Lawrence*：*A Search for Integration*. Columbia, MO. University of Missouri Press. 1971. Print.

Tindall Y. William. "An Introduction to the Latter D. H. Lawrence". 1952. *Twentieth-Century Literary Criticism*. Ed. Dedria Bryfonski. Vol. 2. Gale Research Inc. 1979；356 – 357. Print.

Torgovnick Marianna. "Narrating sexuality：The Rainbow". *D. H. Lawrence*. E-d. Aanne Fernihough. Shanghai：Shanghai Foreign Language Education Press & Cambridge University Press,2003. 33 – 47. Print.

Twentieth-Century Literary Criticism. Ed. Laurie Di Mauro. Vol. 48. Gale Research Inc. 1993. Print.

Undset, Sigrid. "D. H. Lawrence" (1935 – 38). 1939. *Twentieth-Century Literary Criticism.* Ed. Dedria Bryfonski. Vol. 2. Gale Research Inc. 1979: 353 – 354. Print.

Vivas, Eliseo. *D. H. Lawrence: The Failure and the Triumph of Art.* Evanston: Northwestern University Press, 1960. Print.

Voelker C. Joseph. "The Spirit of No-Place: Elements of the Classical Ironic Utopia in D. H. Lawrence's 'Lady Chatterley's Lover'". 1979. *Twentieth-Century Literary Criticism.* Ed. Dennis Poupard. Vol. 9. Gale Research Inc. 1983:227 – 229. Print.

Walters Margeret. Feminism: A Very Short Introduction. New York: Oxford University Press. 2005. Print.

Williams, Linda Ruth. *D. H. Lawrence.* United Kingdom: Northcote House Publishers Ltd. ,1997. 4 – 5. Print.

Wilson, Edmund. "Sign of Life: ' Lady Chatterley's Lover" 1929. *Twentieth-Century Literary Criticism.* Ed. Dedria Bryfonski. Vol. 2. Gale Research Inc. 1979:345. Print.

Worldcat. "Spender, Dale". Web. March, 18th, 2012. < www. worldcat. org >

Wyndham Lewis. *Enemy Salvoes: Selected Literary Criticism.* Ed. C. J. Fox. London: Vision, 1975. 121. Print.

高万隆. 婚恋. 女权. 小说:哈代与劳伦斯小说的主题研究[M]. 中国社会科学出版社. 2009.

葛伦鸿. 查太莱夫人的女性主义解读[J]. 外国文学研究 2 (2001): 41 – 44.

刘 慧. 两性和谐关系背后的阳性论述:重读《查太莱夫人的情人》[J]. 广西师范大学学报:哲学社会科学版 6 (2007):33 – 37.

林语堂. 译者序. 查特莱夫人的情人. 劳伦斯. 林语堂译. 华网书局.

1939. <http://www.abada.cn/top.html>

苗福光. 异化文明的批判与回归自然的主题:析《查特莱夫人的情人》的生态哲学观[J]. 名作欣赏.5（2006）:77 – 80.

裴阳. 人生与社会的断面:恰特莱夫人的情人浅析[J]. 上海外国语学院学报.59,1（1989）:22 – 27.

伍厚凯. 追寻彩虹的人—劳伦斯[M]. 成都:四川人民出版社,1998.

伊丽莎白·莱特. 拉康和后女性主义[M]. 王文华译. 北京:北京大学出版社,2005.

杨文新.《木马赢家》中语言建构的隐含男权. 重庆交通大学学报(社会科学版).3(2016):79 – 83.

杨文新. The View of Marriage in Lady Chatterley's Lover[J]. 海外英语20(2015):156 – 157,164.

王韵秋. 查泰莱夫人的情人中失语女性的解构力量[J]. 山西师大学报(社会科学 版)34,6（2007）:135 – 137.

王琼. 由厌男者到彻底的征服者[J]. 海外文坛6(2011):125 – 128.

张伯香. 英国文学教程[M]. 武汉:武汉大学出版社,1997. 215 – 220.

朱刚. 二十世纪西方文艺批评理论[M]. 上海:上海外语教育出版社,2001.

赵翠华. 白凤欣. D. H. 劳伦斯 查特莱夫人的情人中的血性意识分析[J]. 山东社会科学144,8（2007）:138 – 140.

郑达华. 查特莱夫人的情人哲学层面的思考[J]. 外国文学1(2003):89 – 92.

西蒙·德·波伏娃的《第二性》

——杨文新书评

　　什么是男人？什么是女人？男女有何不同？为何历朝历代男尊女卑的观念根深蒂固？你知道性别和性属的区别和意义吗？你知道男性特质和女性特质是先天的还是后天的吗？你知道男女的发展是否平等了吗？你知道女人是该在家相夫教子，做好母亲、妻子、情人的角色还是应该成为独立女性，有自由选择的权利？……

　　波伏娃的《第二性》将为你解答。《第二性》这本书的内容观点是女性主义的宣言，是两性和谐发展、公平发展的认知读物，也是一本对全世界两性发展和反思影响至深的先驱读物，值得我们大家研读。

　　什么是女人，什么是男人？男性作家本达（Benda）定义道，"男人没有女人可以独立思考，女人没有男人却不行。"在男性眼里，女人不过是"子宫""生命发源地""负面的""不完美的人""附属品"，甚至只不过是"亚当的一根肋骨"；然而在女性眼里，也包括男性，男人却代表着权力、法则、权威、正面的、积极的、优越的，甚至代表着整个人类。对于男性这类一贯的说辞，波伏娃明确告诉我们，两性存在着明显的不平等,"他(男人)是主体,他是绝对,她(女人)却是他者"。

什么是他者?他者是与主体定义相对的概念,也是人类学一个基本的属性。人把自己看作主体,他者也就区别与主体产生了。但主体与他者的概念却没有一开始就与两性相捆绑,也没有依托于任何经验事实。那为何女人会成为他者,被教化成为一个女人,并做一个女人,然后变成一个女人呢?一旦女人想要做出一点改变,女人就会被男人告知她的女性特质正变得岌岌可危。为什么女人常常很欢喜地接受她作为他者的角色,还成为男性的共谋?

一、《第二性》的有力反驳和立论

作者波伏娃在生物学、弗洛伊德的心理学、恩格斯的历史唯物主义和女性历史中寻找以上答案并提出了有利的反驳。她提出,从生物学方面看,男人和女人不存在高低等之分。女人,和男人一样,拥有她自己的身体;但她的身体却又不仅仅是她自己的。当女人从属于后代的繁衍,男人却是自由身,保持着他的个性特征。但身体的这点不同却不能说明是头脑的不同。从心理学方面看,心理学家们根本无法解释"决定论"和"集体无意识"的起源,因此女孩们被剥夺了选择的意识而被要求扮演象征性的女性。波伏娃一语中的,"女人不是天生的,而是变成了女人"。因为女性的自我意识并不是完全受性别决定,而是社会经济组织形式所形成的环境下的一种映射。在恩格斯《家庭、私有财产与国家起源》一书中,波伏娃分析道,尽管恩格斯提出"私有财产的出现是因为男人作为奴隶和土地的拥有者,变成了所有者,也包括对女人。这是女性最大的历史性失败",但恩格斯却没有回答这一切是如何发生的。

波伏娃认为历史的真实性应该用存在主义的观点来解读。在生物学方面,女性对世界探索的欲望少于男性,那是因为女性比男性更加紧密地受制于后代的繁衍。因此当男人一旦获得经济上的主导地位,经济压迫就加深了女性从属地位的社会压迫。"对于男性,她成为了性伴侣、繁衍子嗣的工具、一个欲望的载体——一个他者,一个男性通过此实现自己的他者"。此时,女性尽管受压迫,她却没有失去主体性。此时,她仅仅只被男性视为一个他者(She is only seen as an Other for men)。

而当男性力量、菲勒斯(阴茎)、工具的价值被定义为世界的价值观时,这个基本条件就决定了存在者要通过这个条件来追求自我超越,这时,男性统治的世界出现了。在这个世界,男人一直想掌控女人但女性的主体性威胁、阻碍着男性的统治。为了压制或消除女性的主体性,男人付诸行动,创造了男性价值观,将此作为存在的价值所在。于是女人被男性的价值观左右,逐步变成男性眼中的"女人"。即女性特质的"多种可能性"被男性定义,当女性对这些"可能性"不提出质疑并接受时,她们做了他者,并成为"共谋";她们将无意识地失去自己的主体性,接受被男人定义的他者特性,成为女性他者中的他者(be seen as the Other by men)。她们将帮助男性实现超越,正如文学中被男性作家塑造的女性,要么是个神话,要么带有男性作家的价值观、期望和幻想;在男性语言中,女性扮演着男性超越的角色,最终让男性彰显了自己的男权价值,并潜移默化地影响着女性成为他眼中的女人。

《第二性》明确指出,回到现实,如果有血有肉的女性违背了男性世界所定义的女性特质,即女人该做什么、不该做什么,那么是这个女人错了,而不是他们所定义的女性特质错了。生物学定义了男女性别,但男女的社会属性却不该是先天受男女性别的限制。也就是说,男人和女人有生物学的性别差异,但男性特质和女性特质的分类是由后天社会文化环境决定的。女人应该和男人在社会上有同等地位和选择权,而不是女人一旦选择做了男人做的事,就被认为不是女人,要么受到打压、排挤、惩罚,要么受到不公平的待遇。

波伏娃在书中末尾提出，要解放女性，就要拒绝被男性定义，要拥有自己独立的存在性，男女双方都是主体，双方都可以为另一方保持做一个（社会学上的）他人，肯定双方的差异，男女双方保持"兄弟手足"的关系。

二、《第二性》的阅读意义

《第二性》被称为女性主义"圣经"，它揭露了女性问题的根源——男性的至高无上和女性他者身份在人们意识中的死结。被压迫的带有主体性的女人被男性看作他者，而失去主体性的女人却成为了男人价值观定义中的他者，一个女性他者中的他者。那么读了《第二性》，女人的性属角色该何去何从？这是我们该意识也该反思和解决的问题。

当前性属的发展已经明确提出性属角色由社会文化经济环境决定，不是生理性别的先天绑定。然而性属的平等却不等于法律的平等，在语言、意识、文化等方面，还存在男女性属发展的不平等。女性受到的歧视、压迫、家暴全世界不胜极举；而职业女性面临的不公平待遇、家庭和社会的双重压力，也让职场女性感受到性属平等的路仍然漫长。当前男尊女卑意识在社会上仍在人们的意识、文化、语言中存在，法律外的性属平等仍需一代又一代的你、我、他共同努力捍卫和继续奋斗，教育是必须的。波伏娃的《第二性》、凯特·米丽特的《性政治》、黛儿·斯彭德的《男性制造了语言》等一系列女性主义著作都对性属平等的认识和探讨提供了素材，都让我们醍醐灌顶、不断反思男女平等的现状与发展。社会的和谐，需要男女的和谐，只有人人具备男女性属平等的思想，认同男女性属的平等性，男权思想的根除了，男女真正的平等、和谐和自由发展才会来临，让我们期待这一天并为这一天的到来而努力。

解读《查特莱夫人的情人》中的婚姻观

杨文新

（德宏师范高等专科学校外语系,云南德宏,678400）

摘要:《查特莱夫人的情人》自 1928 年首次出版以来,一直备受争议。作者在小说中呼吁男女之间彻底的性解放,认为这是人类关系的理想平衡。本文系统全面地分析了小说众人物的婚姻,包括康妮的父母、康妮的姐姐、康妮与克里福、梅勒斯和其妻子及理想型夫妇梅勒斯和康妮,由此探讨作者所体现出的婚姻观并对其做出评价。

关键词:婚姻 ；性 ；女性自我意识;爱情

The View of Marriage in *Lady Chatterley's Lover*

Yang Wenxin

（Foreign Languages ' Department,Dehong Teachers' College,678400）

Abstract：Lady Chatterley's Lover has been controversial fiercely since it first published in 1928. In the novel the author calls for a complete emancipation of sex between man and woman,which is the ideal balance of human beings. Systematically and comprehensively,my essay will analyze the characters' marriages,including Connie's parents, her sister, Clifford and Connie,Mellors and his wife,and the ideal couple—Mellors and Connie. Through them,the essay will explore D. H. Lawrence's view of marriage and finally judge the view.

Key words：marriage；sex；female self-consciousness；love

Lady Chatterley's Lover had been controversial fiercely since it first published in 1928. The novel may not the masterpiece with D. H. Lawrence's finest thinking but it is the work for which Lawrence is best known. Until 1960, *Lady Chatterley's Lover* had been accepted and published legally. The reason is that D. H. Lawrence breaks the taboo of the conventional moral ideas and advocates an absolute freedom of sexual expression. The author even calls for a complete emancipation of sex, declaring that any repression of sexual life based on social, religious, or moral values of the civilized world would cause severe damages to the harmony of human relationships and the psychic health of the individual's personality. this frank discussion of sex in his novel is the chief reason why Lawrence has been accused of pornographic writing. [1](p220) However, today, the wider reading public has appreciated the novel in a variety of ways such as from the views of psychology, philosophy, ecology , archetype, naturalism, feminism and etc.

It is a shocking novel with its modernity of styles. Superficially, *Lady Chatterley's Lover* relates the story of a woman called Connie trapped in a marriage with an impotent, insensitive man—Clifford. Her life is sterile and joyless until she finds "phallic tenderness" and sexual fulfillment with an outsider, her gamekeeper—Mellors. Here D. H. Lawrence figured Clifford as a half-man, half-machine husband enslaved by mechanical civilization while Mellors as a "natural aristocrat," [2] with a strong and healthy body, who represents the possible coming of a new order which will transform industrial society into something more humane. The love and future between Mellors and Connie implies an idealistic human relationship between man and woman. In the novel, Mellors is a true man with "blood consciousness" . Through " the touch of tenderness ", he makes Connie reborn from "death", reaching to" balance" between man and women.

1. The Values of the Novel

Lady Chatterley's Lover has been attracting a lot of interest in the worldside for over 80 years. Its charms lie in evoking readers various forms of emotional repulsion. Comprehensively and technically Lawrence not only introduces psychology, imagery, symbolism, realism, romanticism and naturalism in the novel but also focuses his exploration on relationships between men and women, especially those of marriage. Through absolute sexual expression, the novel expresses a Utopian idea—a new world where men and women enjoy true love and freedom, unhampered by social classes, by burdensome family ties, or by ideas of racial and religious superiority after the first world war. The seeking is only a daydream that can not come true because man and society is the most important force to drive the world. However, his understanding of modern consciousness (boredom, irritation, anger, rage, repression, money worship and etc.) and the argument on emancipation of sex indeed anticipate that of many postmodern theorists. That can not be neglected.

2. Analysis & Discussion

Priest(2007) advocates that Lawrence introduces us to the idea that sexual pleasure, for women and for men, is properly a part of marriage—that it is essential to a loving relationship. Today in west people tend to take for granted that sex is a key element of a romantic relationship. It's almost a defining characteristic: if there is no sexual attraction, then no matter what else you feel, you are not 'in love'. He was claiming that it was in sexual intercourse that the true intimacy of a love relationship was enacted. This was a genuinely radical idea at the time. For Lawrence, sex was at the heart of marriage. [3](p58) Is that true? What kind of marriage is happy? How important sex is in marriage? Without sexual pleasure, can the marriage last? Now let's come back into the novel with these questions.

2. 1　Analysis of the Five Couples

The first couple is Connie's parents. In the chapter 1, we saw that Connie's father was an artist well-known R. A. , old Sir Malcolm Reid and her mother was a cultured socialist, one of the cultivate Fabians. Are they happy? The novel writes as follow:

In the last few months of her life, she wanted her girls to be free, and to "fulfill" themselves. She herself had never been able to be altogether herself: it had been denied her. Heaven knows why, for she was a woman who had her own income and her own way. She blamed her husband. But as a matter of fact, it was some old impression of authority on her own mind or soul that she could not get rid of. It had nothing to do with Sir Malcolm, who left his nervously hostile, high-spirited wife to rule her own roost, while he went his own way. [4](p3)

Obviously, Connie's mother is a independent and intelligent woman with strong self-consciousness. She is not satisfied with her marriage. They seem not like a couple: the husband behaves indifferent to her. They are like strangers in the same room and do their things by themselves. The mother realizes the problem between them but the farther does not care. She died and he "got a second wife in Scotland, younger than himself and richer, and he had as many holidays away from her as possible: just as with his first wife. " [4](p190) "Sir Malcolm was always uneasy going back to his wife. It was habit carried over from the first wife. " [4](p204) These words imply Malcolm does not like going home and facing his wives or exactly, he does not love his first wife. In the chapter 18, the idea shows obviously from "Connie was his favorite daughter, he had always liked the female in her. Not so much of her mother in her as in Hilda. " [4](p205) Hilda, like the mother, also has strong self-consciousness. The character blocks love from the man. That can be sure that he dislikes the character in his first wife and daughter.

The second couple is Hilda and her husband. Her husband was " a man ten years older than herself, an elder member of the same Cambridge group, a man with a fair amount of money, and a comfortable family job in the government: he also wrote philosophical essays. " [4] (p4) As the above says, Hilda is like her mother in character. Then, does his husband appreciate her? Are they happy? There is no any remarks about their marriage. They divorce. Why? Through those male spokesman, Sir Malcolm, Clifford and Mellors, the reason is simple: she is "a woman , soft and still as she seemed amazon sort, not made to fit with men" , "an amazon of the real old breed" [4](p54) , "stubborn" and "self-will" [4](p184) . So she deserves what she get: "to be left severely alone. " [4](p184)

The third couple is Connie and Clifford. They married in 1917. After a month's honeymoon, he went back to the army. Six months later, he was shipped over, " more or less in bits " . [4](p1) Through two-year-cure, he "could return to life with the lower half of his body, from the hips down, paralysed for ever. " [4](p1) Connie was then 23 and "the war had brought the roof down over her head. " [4](p1) How can they keep their marriage? Losing the right of sex, Clifford only showed the other talents to attract his young wife. He published many "curious and meaningless" stories and essays, which made him earn a lot of money and also promote fame. First, Connie was tempted into helping his writing. Gradually, she felt empty, hopeless and painful to life. She met Michaelis. When she was ready to divorce his husband and marry him, she found he was also a hypocritical man. Then her husband started to try how to manage his mine field. When he enjoyed his accomplishments, his wife became desperate and hated his everything. She was slowly dying. At that time, Mellors' "tenderness of touch" helped Connie escape from "death" and get "rebirth". Finally she made a decision to divorce and start a new life with Mellors. In her eyes, her husband, half-man and half-machine, was enslaved by money and mechanical civilization while only Mellors was a true man who could make her refreshed and happy. The balls decide masculine nature? The idea is ridiculous. Ellis tells us it is the nature of society that cultivates masculine qualities but not the amounts of semen. Otherwise, the true manly nature embodies how to treat the female including how to love her considerately, to please and tease her, and to feel the need in emotion and physiology. [5](p124) So the problem between Connie and Clifford is obvious: first, no sexual pleasure; second, no spiritual resonance. So their marriage is doomed to be a failure.

The fourth couple is Mellors and Bertha Coutts. According to the narration, Bertha Coutts was rude to Mellors. "she treated me with insolence. And she got so's she'd never have me when I wanted her: never. Always put me off, brutal as you like. And then when she'd put me right off, and I didn't want her, lovey-dovey, and get me. " [6](p149) Mellors hated her and so did her. After their child was born, he left her alone and she was with another man. Their marriage is also a failure. The reason is that Mellors hates his wife's dominating consciousness in sex.

The fourth marriages above are not happy. What kind of marriage is happy? The author directs us that Connie and Mellors will be a happy couple in the novel. Connie, tender, obedient and passionate to her lover, is different from her mother, her sister and Bertha Coutts who are masculine women and not fascinated by the men in the novel. She is a true woman, the ideal type a true man loves. And the true man was Mellors, strong, healthy, far from the civilization of mechanism. According to the author, their combination is the ideal balance between man and woman. They enjoy sexual pleasure and freedom, unhampered by social classes, by burdensome family ties, or by ideas of racial and religious superiority.

" it's tenderness, really; it's cunt-awreness. Sex is really touch, the closest of all touch. And it's touch we're afraid of . We're only haf-conscious, and half alive. We 've got to come alive and aware. Especially the English have got to get into touch with one another, a bit delicate and a bit tender. It's our crying need. " [4](p208)

For Lawrence, sex was the closest touch of human being. So men and women need the touch of sex and the society's development also needs the touch. Sex was at the heart of marriage. In that case, without sex, the marriage is doomed to die. These exaggerated words are unreasonable.

2. 2　Sex , Love and Marriage

Everyone, whether man or woman, is unique and equal. If the ideal society is only full of one type of women (Connie) or men(Mellors) , it is too dull. The novel ends, leaving the couple waiting, apart, for the various entanglements of their previous marriages to be sorted out. As Lyon(1920) says, Lawrence's own life suggests that the problem of finding of a " new world" is one that, in his life as in his art, he never solved. [6]

Besides, marriage needs respect and understanding between husband and wife on the basis of love. Sexual pleasure is part of marriage, which can not be the most important part. Havelock Ellis was a pioneering sex psychologist in the first decade of the twentieth century and a respected English literary figure. The Chinese version of his works by Yang Dongxiong is titles as *Happiness Code*, which has been published in 2004. For sex, he is objective and scientific. His view has been acknowledged by the world. In *Happiness Code*, Ellis points out that marriage's aim should be reflection of love. In the late marriage, the element of sex will slowly decrease and finally quit. Love will support the relationships of family.

Then what is love? Abu Muhammad Ibn Hazm (994 – 1064 a. d.) has defines *the* Concept of Love as follows:

Its true nature cannot be described in words. It can only be realized through personal experience. It starts at the sight of a beautiful face, because by nature man is attracted towards good-looking objects. But that is only the preliminary stage of love. It thrives and grows into its second and more important stage only when the lover finds some spiritual affinity beyond the physical charms of the beloved. That affinity is reflected through similarity in natural disposition of both the lover and the beloved. If such spiritual attraction is not found, the liking felt for the physical charms can never develop into love. If anyone continues with such liking, he has nothing to do with love. He only indulges in lust. It is also described as cheap love. While all cases of cheap love soon end in disaster, real love lasts permanently. [7]

Abu Muhammad Ibn Hazm clearly identifies love and sex here. Marriage needs real love but not cheap love (sex). Everyone is not perfect. It is love that makes man and woman understand and tolerant each other. So the marriage with love is happy and the marriage without love will be very difficult to last. Besides, equality between man and woman is also important. On the basis of equality, love can work better.

3. Conclusion

Through comprehensively analyzing the five marriages of the characters in the novel, my essay deduces that sex is important element in marriage but not the dominating one; love is the key between man and women, and also the key in marriage; in the novel, the male always take the lead. Connie's mother, her sister and Bertha Coutts are not loved by the male in the novel because they have strong self-consciousness. They are not true women but masculine women. Only Connie is a tender and true woman. Here the definition Lawrence makes the ideal female is one-side, full of the masculine tone of himself. to the question that how the future between the ideal couple, Connie and Mellors, was, the author himself could not answer. He terminated his narrative before more contradictions emerges. His vision of the future was not always clear. In the novel, Lawrence's bias towards women with strong female-consciousness and his unreasonable view of marriage on the basis of the bias are very obvious. However, certainly he recognized that suppressing sexual feelings would not make life any more bearable. "Though he may not offer any easy solutions, he certainly helped remove the blinders that had prevented people from facing squarely that sexual relationships were basic to being human. "[8] That is the positive value of the novel.

Works Cited:

1. 张伯香. 英国文学教程[M]. 武汉:武汉大学出版社,1997:220.

2. Koh,J. K. D. H. Lawrence's world vision of cultural regeneration in Lady Chatterley's Lover[J]. *The Midwest Quarterl*,2002,43,(2).

3. Priest, A. M. Married sex: Ann-Marie Priest highlights the importance of

D. H. Lawrence as a proselytiser for the role of sex in love and marriage[J]. *Meanjin* 66. 1 (2007):58.

4. Lawrence D. H. . Lady Chatterley's Lover [M]. China's External Economic Trade Press. Beijing:2000.

5. 爱丽斯. 幸福密码[M],杨东雄译. 喀什:喀什维吾尔出版社,2004.

6. Lyon,J. M. Lady Chatterley's Lover:Overview[A]. *Reference Guide to English Literature*. Ed. D. L. Kirkpatrick. 2nd ed. Chicago:St. James Press,1991.

7. Ali,A. Ibn Hazm as Moralist and Interpreter of Love[J]. *Hamdard Islamicus* 18. 3 (Fall 1995):77 – 84.

8. Martin, M. S. . D. H. Lawrence:Overview [A]. *Gay & Lesbian Literature*. Vol. 1. Detroit:Gale,1994.

（该文发表于《海外英语》2015 年第 20 期）

Appendix 3

《木马赢家》中语言所建构的隐含男权

杨文新

（德宏师范高等专科学校外语系，云南，芒市，678400）

摘要：《木马赢家》是劳伦斯晚期著名的短篇小说。该小说被拍成了影片，还被选进了校园课本，其影响非常巨大。小说讲述了小男孩保罗之死的故事，也因为小男孩的死，对母亲海斯特的评论大都持负面批判态度，却对父亲的"不在场"所隐含的男权关注甚少。细细分析文本，发现保罗之死与母亲并没有绝对的关系，而是小说中语言所形成的"男权象征体系"误导了读者，而将母亲推向了审判席。

关键词：《木马赢家》；隐含男权；语言；保罗；母亲；父亲的"不在场"

中图分类号：I106.4I 文献标识码：A 文章编号：1674 – 0297 (2016)03 – 0079 – 0

The Implied Patriarchy Made by Language in The Rocking-Horse Winner

YANG Wenxin

(Department of Foreign Languages, Dehong Teachers' College,
Mangshi, Yunnan 678400, China)

Abstract: The Rocking-Horse Winner is a famous short fiction of Lawrence's late works, which produces a great influence on people after being made into movie and selected into school and university curricula. The fiction tells a story about the death of a little boy named Paul. Just due to his death, most criticisms on the mother, Hester, hold the negative views but less analyzed the implied patriarchy by the father's "absence". The essay scrutinizes the text, finding out Paul's death is not absolutely related to his mother but the "patriarchal order"—a symbolic order made in the language of the fiction, misleads readers and pushes the mother to the judgment seat.

Key words: The Rocking-Horse Winner; implied Patriarchy; language; Paul; Mother; Father's "absence"

《木马赢家》是劳伦斯 1926 年发表的短篇小说,在被英国导演安东尼·佩利西耶1950年搬上美国屏幕后,影响剧增。当然,该小说的影响深远与弗兰克·雷蒙德·里维斯等人将其一系列作品推广进入中学校园和大学教学大纲中也密不可分。

该短篇小说讲述了一个叫保罗的男孩,为了向母亲证明自己的财运,背地里疯狂地约着园丁巴塞特和舅舅奥斯卡投入到赛马场的赌博中。由于每一次押注前,保罗都要骑在自己的玩具木马上寻求所谓上帝的明示,不停摇晃,并挥舞皮鞭,最终殚精竭虑,结束了自己的生命。死时,他留下了八万英镑的赌资。该小说悲剧性的结尾,与劳伦斯晚期思想所要批判的一脉相承,都是直指工业社会给人带来的金钱崇拜、物质崇拜和最终的人性毁灭。在这些社会主题下,作者也把读者和评论者的视线引到了对母亲的批判上。

母亲的贪婪、无情、自私、爱慕虚荣、贪图享受都要为保罗的死——买单[1][2][3]。而父亲的"不在场"引发的只是俄狄浦斯情结的一系列分析。像陈兵就从俄狄浦斯情结分析指出,对《木马赢家》中母亲海斯特的负面刻画有特殊意义,意义在于对西方现代文明的否定,也如里弗(Reeve)所言,旨在让我们更尊重父亲权威统治下的传统家庭观[4]。杨彩霞则只关注父亲的"缺席"对保罗恋母情结悲剧的影响[5]。

为什么父亲"不在场"？如果将母亲的角色和父亲互换,一样可以达到文章要批判的意义。为何母亲就成了"保罗之死"的元凶？

一、语言体系的象征作用

女性主义者认为,小说作为意识形态的一种强有力的工具,拥有"对想象力颠覆性的力量"[6]132。黛儿·斯彭德(Dale Spender)指出,女性们一直都意识到男性的优越是个神话,而这个神话并不与男性权利挂钩,而是付诸于语言这个象征系统。正是男性利用语言创造了一个以男人为主的象征秩序,"一个男权至上的秩序",才使我们进入到这样的秩序所代表的意义,继而一代代相承,不断使之实现。这样的秩序即使不合理,但在语言体系的象征作用下,如果不对此警惕和有所行动,我们终将处在"一个性别系统中",最终看到的还是男权至上的秩序,"处处有父权制"[7]5-9。

因此,尽管小说有着丰富的社会主题,但对母亲的负面刻画和对父亲的"不在场"处理却继续威胁着男女性属平等的建立。小说中隐含男权的思想应引起读者和评论者的注意,尤其是教师对学生的课堂讲授和分析。同时也要注意到劳伦斯的作品并不是孤立的,它们一脉相承,不仅体现了他对西方工业文明的控诉、人与人关系的异化、男女关系平衡的探讨,也展露着他对男权思想的追求。

二、劳伦斯男权思想路线

劳伦斯早期作品,《白孔雀》(1911)、《闯入者》(1912)和《儿子与情人》(1913)都是他早期有代表意义的作品。这些作品都不太成熟,仅仅展示了他年轻时的一些经历以及他和父母关系的一些问题。在这一阶段,劳伦斯只是一个"永远的妈妈男孩"[8]249。

为摆脱母亲的影响,他相继和一些女人发生恋爱或性关系,最终与有夫之妇的弗里达结成连理,并将他们的关系作为蓝本探讨男女关系。这一阶段他创作了《虹》(1915)和《恋爱中的女人》(1920)。但他一直深受男权思想的影响,虽一直想协调男女关系使之平衡,却没有在这个缓和阶段协调成功。正如波伏娃一语道破的,一方面劳伦斯提出男性的狂妄自大会激起女性的抵抗,只有双方毫无统治欲望的"相互的支配"(the reign of mutuality)才能达到完美的平衡;一方面他却没有构建出这样的支配,女主人公遵从了男主人公的想法,被他统治,被他拯救[9]247-248。

后劳伦斯直接进入到了一个极端典型的男权思想阶段。在其作品《阿伦的拐杖》(1922),《袋鼠》(1923),《羽蛇》(1926),《无意识幻想曲》中,我们可以看到男性都被创造成主角,都是男性世界的领导者;他们拒绝女性进入世界的权利;在个人关系上,都要求女性对男性绝对的服从。

到了后期,劳伦斯在经历了第一次世界大战的颠沛流离和对女权运动引发的两性之争后,尤其又深受病痛的折磨,面临妻子的出轨,在写作上更偏重于人性毁灭的主题;在两性探讨上,如《查特莱夫人的情人》中,虽不那么极端,但劳伦斯还是把康妮塑造成了一个"性爱被动"的女子,一个"女性意志被放弃"的人[10]113-115[11]370[12]411-413[13]356-357,一个视"梅勒斯为上帝般权威"的女人,一个"他者"[9]245-254。

总之,劳伦斯更主张女人的角色应该是母亲、妻子和情人,像母鸡一样温顺,懂得下蛋、孵蛋即可,别妄图成为公鸡,参与投票、从政、外出就业等活动[14]125-127。男人应该做自己屋子的主人[14]99-101。其作品一直都在为男权思想的象征体系服务。

三、《木马赢家》中的隐含男权

由上可知,《木马赢家》发表于1926年,其思想路线进入明显的男权阶段。但由于故事主角是小男孩,情节是小男孩之死,故让许多读者在故事情节中理所当然地追究保罗为什么会死。矛头自然而然对准母亲。因为故事中,父亲像个隐身人,一个旁观者。他没有和孩子有过交流,也没文字提到他对孩子的关心,保罗死前的那一夜,母亲忧心忡忡地冲上楼去看,而他在楼下调制威士忌苏打酒。死时,母亲、舅舅、园丁都在场,独独没有他。也没任何人说起他。而作者却借舅舅奥斯卡之口,将保罗之死的责任推向母亲。"我的上帝。海斯特,你赢了八万多英镑,却输了可怜的儿子。但是可怜的孩子,可怜的孩子,他走得好,不用过骑木马找赢家的生活了"[15]197。是他的母亲害的他吗?他的父亲呢?他的"不在场"就可以逃离责任吗?

(一)谁该为保罗的死负责?

保罗是因为心力交瘁,急于要知道马赛谁会赢,而赌上了自己的性命。他为什么会迷上马赛?作者在故事开头插入了一段保罗和母亲的对话,这个对话也是许多读者,包括学生认为的证据。对话一开始,是孩子保罗问母亲为什么我们没有车,要用舅舅家的,而不是母亲对孩子抱怨没有车。这一点可以说明,当时工业经济的发展、物质的丰富,使得人人都想努力拥有或攀比的社会现象已经深入人心,连保罗这么小的孩子都对物质的追求和拥有觉得理所应当。这是整个社会风气的影响,人人都深陷其中,包括这个家庭的所有人。

在母亲解释为什么没有钱买车,是因为父亲没有运气之后,保罗又问他的母亲,舅舅奥斯卡所说的"filthy lucker"是不是钱。这里,保罗把"lucre"理解成了"luck-er"。而母亲明确解释了"lucre"是钱,不是运气。然而保罗之后的行为却仍然将赛马得来的"filthy lucre"当做自己的运气。如果说是母亲误导了保罗,那么从这里可以看出,是保罗没有明白母亲的意思,而坚持自己的认知。而这个错误认知的来源可以明确的是来自舅舅奥斯卡。

再者,作者一开始就告诉我们"这里有个美丽的女人,一开始具备各种优势,然而她却没有运气"[15]177。母亲的没运气,导致她婚后收入微薄,嫁的丈夫也收入低,他们入不敷出,为此,母亲绞尽脑汁想办法,但没有成功。母亲最后在城里画皮装和衣料赚钱,但却无法像她朋友一样成功,一年只能挣朋友的十分之一——几百英镑。即使母亲如此没运气,母亲也没参与赛马赌博或其他不正当的手段来赚钱。而保罗的参与赛马也一直瞒着母亲,当母亲隐约感知到儿子的不正常时,也说过,"这是个不好的预兆。我的家庭是个好赌的家庭,等你长大了才会知道它的坏处有多大……"[15]195。这些都足以证明母亲并没有误导儿子去赚不义之财就是运气,而是保罗自以为是的越走越错。

那么在保罗走错的路上,他的母亲是不知道的,父亲也不"在场",在场的是园丁巴塞特和舅舅奥斯卡。作为成年男性,巴塞特没有制止保罗的行为,也没有及时告知他的父母,相反,帮助他一次次赌马,即使有输有赢,也坚信保罗有"运气",有上帝的指示。作为舅舅,奥斯卡对侄子听之任之、助之,最终将其毁之,却在侄子死时,将责任推得一干二净,认为这一切都是海斯特这个母亲造成的。这两个成年男性的行为和想法多么的理所当然,他们这样做似乎是在帮保罗,帮保罗获得母亲的爱或着关注。有着这样的借口,就可推脱责任吗?显然作者并无意让母亲开口辩解,一切在舅舅奥斯卡的指责中结束。这种男权思想的一派作风却将母亲这个角色推到批判的风口浪尖。而作为帮凶的巴塞特和奥斯卡却成为圆可怜男孩梦想的伪道夫!而"不在场"的父亲更是一点关系都没有,从头到尾都没他什么事!故事中用语言所构建的这个象征秩序,维护了男性至上的权益,却将女性打入了原罪的批判席。作者的目的不外乎告诫女性,当好母亲的角色,不要追求家庭之外的事。否则,你的追求到头来,"什么都不是"(Nothingness)[14]127。

(二)母亲海斯特

海斯特是个美丽的女人,因为爱情而结的婚,婚后爱情却"化成灰烬了"[15]177。如果将这作为海斯特没有爱,无情、冷酷的开始,似乎不合情理。现实生活中,女人婚前对爱情的幻想离不开男人婚前浪漫贴心的承诺,但婚后,生活的柴米油盐开支、养育儿女的艰辛和劳累,男人语言及行为的反差等等无不让女人操心、焦虑、担忧甚至抑郁。这些都是普遍的心理现象,不足为据。

作者接着叙述,"她有几个很好的孩子,然而她觉得这些孩子是强加在她头上的,她不能(could not)爱他们"[15]177。"could not"和"did not"是有区别的。一个是能力上的不能,一个是否定的没有。显然母爱是天性,作者都没有否认这种天性,却有读者会错意了。她不能爱他们,原因在于,"他们冷冷地看着她,好像在找她的茬"[15]177。孩子是调皮的、任性的,需要大人耐心管教的。海斯特有三个孩子,一个男孩保罗,两个女孩。虽有仆人帮忙,但从整个故事可以看出,对家庭的责任感、对孩子的责任感,海斯特都比丈夫投入得多。因此她情感上产生了分裂。一方面,她内心深处不能感觉到爱(could not feel love),也感觉不到对任何人的爱;一方面,责任感又要迫使她去关心她的孩子,爱她的孩子。这种分裂,孩子和母亲双方都清楚。爱是双方的,海斯特感觉不到孩子的爱,丈夫的爱,而责任上她必须爱他们。这种分裂合乎情理。

当然,对女性这种婚后情感如此细微和真实的描述不得不说是劳伦斯写作的一大特色。有评论者就曾认为劳伦斯就是一个女人,如诺曼·梅勒和开罗·迪克斯。他们就认为他是肉体上的男性,精神上的女性[16]266。但劳伦斯毕竟是个男性作家,骨子里的男性作家。为此,辛普森(Simpson)认为,"从评论争议之初,对劳伦斯厌女症的攻击以及赞扬他对女性特质感性地描述,就一直并存"[17]13。

接着,作者交代海斯特的家是一个带花园的房子,他们有仆人,也觉得(felt)他们自己在邻里来说比别人优越[15]177。但他们的收入微薄,无法满足他们所要维持的社会地位的开销。于是,他们感到(felt)一种焦虑。劳伦斯反复使用"felt",这里要表达的是一种主观情感,作者意指他们为了面子,为了追求物质享受,为了攀比而自寻烦恼。

由此可见,整个家庭情感上都笼罩在这样的焦虑中,他们需要更多的钱,但他们没有钱。对此,母亲海斯特费尽心思想办法,但都不成功,失败使她长满皱纹。而作为父亲,虽在城里任职,前景也好,但总是无法实现。家里缺钱，父亲并没有为此烦恼，相反，"风度翩翩，出手阔绰，似乎从来不会做一些有意义的事"[15]178。

在缺钱的情况下，海斯特最后去城里画皮装和衣料赚钱。这一点，有评论者赞誉母亲没有放弃希望，"突围"困境[18]。但还是缺钱。缺钱的呼声响彻整个家庭，保罗也想"突围"。前面已经分析过，保罗赛马赌博行为与母亲的对话没有绝对关系，在赌马过程中，母亲也是不知道的。但保罗赢得的钱是要给母亲。为什么给母亲？

整个故事，只有母亲在履行责任，而父亲是"不在场"的。保罗在母亲生日给母亲的钱，虽然母亲一次性领取了，但说她贪婪、自私，似乎不合理。母亲并没有把钱自己挥霍，相反"家里有了一些新家具，保罗有了家庭教师"[15]194。而母亲在保罗有异样时，也对保罗担心、焦虑、恐慌。在最终发现保罗的秘密时，已经来不及了。

保罗死时问母亲，"妈妈，我告诉过你吗？我是幸运的！""不，你从来没有说过，"母亲答道[15]197。保罗有说过，当母亲说她确实不走运时。当时母亲笑笑，保罗"自己也不知道为什么这么说"[15]179。之后就像为了证明他说的是真的，他开始了赛马生涯。前后两个对话的呼应，责任直指母亲。可仔细阅读，这样的指责是否不够有力。母亲理解的运气，和保罗自己认定的运气并不一致。母亲说，"如果你是富有的，你或许会失去钱财。但如果你是幸运的，你将一直会有更多的钱"[15]178-179。保罗第一次赌马输了，他就应该及时制止自己的错误。但他接着用舅舅奥斯卡给的10先令去赌，赢了，为此他自我欺骗式的相信舅舅运气一定好，自己和巴塞特的运气也好，"因为是用你给的10先令我才开始赢的……"[15]182。

最后便是奥斯卡舅舅板上钉钉的话，"我的上帝。海斯特，你赢了八万多英镑，却输了可怜的儿子。但是可怜的孩子，可怜的孩子，他走得好，不用过骑木马找赢家的生活了"[15]197。讽刺的是，奥斯卡在孩子昏厥中听到孩子所说的赛马名字,还有心情赌上了 1000 英镑赌注。作者要讽刺人性的毁灭,这里奥斯卡、巴塞特的人性比母亲海斯特更加罪恶、麻木、自私和无情。

可是,谁赋予了奥斯卡说出这样的话? 而母亲只是魂不守舍,像个石头一般无法思考,一句话也没有说。母亲的不言不代表整个指控就是合理的,就是真的。黛儿·斯彭德(Spender Dale)在《男性制定的语言》一书中就明确指出,我们要构建两性平等,如果在"男权象征体系"的一系列语言中,我们没有能力辨认和改变这些象征意义,那么我们就沦为了帮助男权继续成为神话的帮手。永远都是"男性是正的,女性是负的"[7]8-9。

(三)父亲的"不在场"

整个故事,除了开头交代了有父亲这么一个人存在,对于家庭,对于孩子,他似乎置身事外,包括保罗死时,他也没有出现。为什么会这样? 合情合理吗? 不合理! 那作者把父亲写成"不在场",目的何在?

如果如里弗(Reeve)所言,劳伦斯旨在让我们更加尊重父亲权威统治下的传统家庭观[4]88;那么劳伦斯的男权思想昭然若揭。因为他一直认为,男人应当做自己领地的主人,不管是在家还是在外[14]99-101,103-106;如果被女性夺取了,正如故事中海斯特负责着整个家,那就是"身份认同危机"[19]155,是一种"反常的过程"[20]141。他认为现在女性外出就业,不安心做家庭主妇,对社会既不自然也不健康。按照作者的思想论调,《木马赢家》中父亲的"不在场"就是一种有意而为之的行为了。

可笑的是,整个故事不改变情节,如果母亲海斯特的角色和父亲互换,母亲变成"不在场",这样的悲剧一样会发生,有何不同? 恐怕,不同在于父亲将成为那个替罪羔羊,批判的呼声不会逊于"不在场"的母亲,而这样的结果不是作者乐见的。

一如前面分析的,父亲的"不在场"同样应当为保罗和这个家庭的悲剧负责,置身事外不代表就不需要批判。家庭和孩子,他同样有着不可推卸的责任。把孩子和家庭推给女性,认为是女性不应当甩脱的责任,这种男权思想至今存在。女性在工作和家庭双重压力下,寻求性属平等的路还很长。而对带有这种思想的语言不加批判,为性属平等所付出的努力必将更加充满阻碍。波伏娃在1976年的访谈中就说道,法律的平等不等于性属的平等,为此,"女性应该明白,即使处于阶级斗争中,阶级斗争也不会消除性别之间的斗争"[21]。

四、结语

《木马赢家》中劳伦斯通过保罗迷于赛马赌博赚钱以示运气,最终从自己的木马上摔下而亡的故事,深刻揭露了人性在一味追求物质、金钱上的毁灭,这是值得肯定和歌颂的。但故事中的语言却有意将保罗之死直指母亲海斯特。对她大加指责的文字评论可见一斑,其影响不可小觑。再者《木马赢家》早已进入教材,作为受众的学生也常常会被误导。本文分析了该小说中语言所带有的隐含男权,意在解读和欣赏此小说时,能客观、公正地对作者的思想、小说的人物,尤其是女主人公海斯特,做出合理的批判和评价。

参考文献

[1]欧 荣.《木马赛冠军》:一则现代寓言[J].浙江万里学院学报,2006(3):: 31－34.

[2]李 烨.《木马赢家》中少年保罗形象的意义探析[J].吉林省教育学院学报, 2010(01):132－133.

[3]吴小英.《木马赢家》中保罗之死的原因[J].安顺学院学报,2012(5): 31－33.

[4]陈兵.劳伦斯《木马赢家》中的俄狄浦斯情结问题[J].解放军外国语学院学报,2011(3):85－89.

[5]杨彩霞. 试论《木马赢家》中父亲形象的缺席[J]. 文教资料,2009(1)上旬 38 – 39.

[6]Seldon Raman,Winddowson Peter and Brooker Peter. *A Reader's Guide to Contemporary Literary Theory*[M]. Beijing:Foreign Language Teaching and Research Press,2004.

[7]Spender Dale. *Man Made Language* [M]. Routledge & Kegan Paul,1980.

[8] Ruderman, Judith. "Lawrence Among the Women: Wavering Boundaries in Women's Literary Traditions" [J]. *Studies in the Novel* 25. 2 (1993):249 +.

[9] Beauvoir de Simone. *The Second Sex* [M] .Trans. H Parshley. London: Vintage,1997.

[10]Bedient,Calvin. "The Radicalism of 'Lady Chatterley's Lover",1966. *Twentieth-Century Literary Criticism* [M]. Ed. Dedria Bryfonski and Sharon K. Hall. Vol. 2. Gale Research Inc. 1979:370 – 371.

[11] Rudikoff, Sonya. "D. H. Lawrence and Our Life Today" [J]. *Commentary*, 28 (1959):408 – 413.

[12] Tindall Y. William. "An Introduction to the Latter D. H. Lawrence" . 1952. *Twentieth-Century Literary Criticism* [M] . Ed. Dedria Bryfonski. Vol. 2. Gale Research Inc. 1979:356 – 357.

[13] Squires, Michael. "The Creation of Lady Chaterley's Lover. " 1983. *Twentieth-Century Literary Criticism* [M] . Ed. Laurie Di Mauro. Vol. 48. Gale Research Inc. 1993: 129 – 134.

[14] Lawrence, D. H. , *Late Essays And Articles* [M] , Ed. James T. Boulton, United Kingdom:Cambrige University Press. 2004.

[15]Lawrence,D. H. ,*The Rocking-Horse Winner*. Extensive Reading 2 [M] ,Ed. Liu Naiyin,Higher Education Press. 2011:177 – 182,191 – 197.

[16] Baldick,Chris. "Lawrence's Critical and Cultural legacy". *D. H. Lawrence* [M] . Ed. Aanne Fernihough. Shanghai:Shanghai Foreign Language Education Press & Cambridge University Press,2003:253 – 268.

[17]Simpson,Hilary. *D. H. Lawrence and Feminism*[M]. Groom Helm Ltd,1982.

[18]黄慧慧. 困境与突围——劳伦斯《木马赢家》解读[J]. 江苏教育学院学报

（社会科学）2011（2）:125 – 127.

[19] Kermode,Frank. *Modern Essays*[M]. London:Fontana Press,1990.

[20]Lawrence,D. H. *Fantasia of the Unconscious and Psychoanalysis and the Unconscious*[M]. Great Britain:Penguin Books,1971.

[21]Beauvoir de Simone. "The second sex 25 years later" – the interview with Simone de Beauvoir by John Garassi. Southapton University. 1976.

（注:该文已发表于《重庆交通大学学报》社会科学版 2016 年第三期）

Appendix 4

议劳伦斯性属观点在作品中的发展与变化

杨文新

内容摘要：劳伦斯是 20 世纪最富争议的作家之一，他对性属问题所持的观点一直备受争议。他是"双性同体"的赞成者，也是男女性属角色极端两级化的提出者，同时又矛盾地想两者兼有。本文从他四个阶段的主要作品、哲学思想和人生经历出发，探讨劳伦斯性属观点的发展与变化，最后得出作为男性作家，劳伦斯在意识和语言上所持的男女性属观点其实一直在追求男性的主体地位和意义，他并未平衡好男女的性属角色，性属的平等还有很长的路要奋斗。

关键词：性属平等；男人；女人；劳伦斯；作品；男性意义

Gender Views' Development and Change in Lawrence's Works

Yang Wenxin

Abstract: D. H. Lawrence is one of the twentieth-century's most controversial novelists, whose views on gender has always been disputed. He not only argued the similar view to "androgyny", but also held the extremely man-woman split view. Even contradictorily both of them. The essay, listing his main works, ideas of the four periods and experiences as a whole, studies his development and change in gender views , finding out more clearly that being a male writer, Lawrence, without balancing the gender roles of both sexes, was still pursuing and building the dominating status and significance of man in his ideology and language. And it has a long way to struggle for the gender equality.

Key Words: Gender equality; man; woman; Lawrence; Works ; the Significance of Man

戴维德·赫伯特·劳伦斯(1885 – 1930)是 20 世纪最有争议性的作家之一,他的作品涉猎面广,有长篇、中篇和短篇小说,也有诗集、散文、翻译、戏剧和画作。但与同时代的艾兹拉·庞德、T. S. 艾略特、詹姆斯·乔伊斯和弗吉尼亚·伍尔夫相比,劳伦斯在文学上的地位"有时,似乎远远比上不他们的稳定。"[1]3在他的作品中,他总是自由表达关于政治、婚姻、社会、教育、宗教以及男人和女人的一些极端看法,常常通过叙述男女间的性。因此,正如托格夫尼克一语道破的:"每个人在一开始,都会感到这样的需要,要么喜欢劳伦斯,要么讨厌他"[1]33。对于喜欢他的人来说,如 E. M. 福斯特、F. R. 里维斯、雷蒙德·威廉姆斯和理查德·霍加特,就认为劳伦斯是一个天才、一个预言家或者文化偶像。而对于不喜欢劳伦斯的人来说,他就是一个最具争议性的作家。如艾略特早早就表示,"劳伦斯的生活就如一个故事,充满着精神上的骄傲、情感上的病态、自我式的欺骗和某种无知。这些缺陷即使是剑桥学者,也无法弥补"[1]257。女性主义者也有同感。此外,作为20 世纪的作家,劳伦斯无论是过去还是现在,都常常被主流作家们,包括詹姆斯·乔伊斯和弗吉尼亚·伍尔夫看作"现代主义的边缘"。但正是这种相对边缘化的位置,反而促使劳伦斯成为"评论中心"的作家[1]179。到目前为止,关于他的书籍和册子就达 650 本之多,而论文已达数万篇。对于这个现象,艾略特早就评论说,"关于谈论劳伦斯的各种书籍所给的印象就是,他是一个通过阅读要去了解的人而不是一个要去阅读的作家"[1]220。原因就在于劳伦斯的作品一直都与他的经历和哲学分不开,它们就像一个三联体。

　　劳伦斯的三联体特点使其作品和形成的哲学思想带上了浓郁的个人经历色彩,尤其是对男女性属角色的观点研究备受争议。他是"双性同体"的赞成者,也是男女性属角色极端两级化的提出者,同时也矛盾地两者兼有。本文将从他人生经历所形成的四个阶段的作品和哲学思想出发,分析作者所持的性属观点的变化来探讨性属平等的问题。

一、影响劳伦斯作品和思想的主要人生经历

劳伦斯一直都是在用他的生活背景和人生经历做写作原材料。对于这一点,评论家们都无异议。劳伦斯出生于工人家庭,父亲是一个目不识丁的煤矿工人,母亲曾当过教师。常年生活在伊斯威特矿村,劳伦斯一直都憎恨那些黑黑的矿区。因次,首先由工业文明所导致的环境污染和人性机械化的场景反复出现在他的作品中。

此外,他父母的婚姻关系也是影响他作品和个人的一个重要因素。他的母亲,利迪娅·比尔兹尔是工程师的女儿,来自中产阶级家庭,当过教师。父亲则是一个矿工兼文盲,身体强健但脾气暴躁。据劳伦斯在《论美国文学名著》中描述,他的父亲"憎恨书籍、憎恨任何人阅读或书写的场面";而母亲则是"憎恨让她的任何一个儿子注定干体力活的想法。她的儿子必须做高档一点的事"[2]。他们几乎没有什么共同语言,婚姻可以说是灾难性的。对于他们,劳伦斯有着复杂的情感。正如他的自传体小说《儿子与情人》中描述的一样。首先,他深爱他的母亲,依赖她的一切并憎恨他的父亲。然后随着年龄的成熟,他慢慢尝试摆脱母亲对他的影响和控制,开始一步步接受并喜欢上自己的父亲。对于劳伦斯,按照他对女性的分类,他的母亲一直都是一个"公鸡般自负的女人"[3]。因此,他对母亲,既爱又怕,想要依赖她又想逃离她。这也影响到了他对其他女性的态度。一方面,他讨厌"占有欲强的女人"或者"公鸡般自负的女人";而另一方面,他也感到她们比起男人要有力量的多(弗里达 Frieda)[4]。在他的创作中,男人和女人的关系,尤其在婚姻中,一直都是他竭力想要去挖掘的主题。通常来讲,他双亲的婚姻是灾难性的,却"诞生了 D. H. 劳伦斯"[5]。

第三,影响他的作品的因素,还有他和女性们(像杰西·钱伯斯、露伊·巴罗斯、爱丽丝·达克斯等等)的性经历,尤其是和妻子弗里

达。根据与他相关生平的介绍,他年轻时的性意识长期受母亲的权威
和基督教教义压制,进入大学后,在阅读了达尔文和尼采的激进书籍
后,性对他成为一种崭新的体验(高 ;Priest)[6-7]。通过性,年轻的他
成功地放下了对母亲情感的迷恋,开始独立地追寻"两性来说,我是
谁?"(托格夫尼克 Torgovnick)[1] 33这也是在他的整个写作中为什么如
此关注性主题的原因。通过性,他开创性地诠释了男人和女人或性属
角色的意义。

第四,他处于第一次世界大战和两性之战的年代,他一直"将人类
的毁灭归于对征服的欲望——征服自然、征服肉体、征服伴侣、征服下
层阶级、征服对手国家以及征服抵触个人意志和集体意志的一切"(桑
德 Sander)[8]。

而他的疾病——肺结核也是一个迫使他发掘该双重主题——死
亡-重生的部分原因。对于这一主题,正如桑德(Sander)指出的,对
于劳伦斯来说,上面这些对征服的追求都建立在"分离的错觉"中,都
误以为"意识可以和身体分离;自我可以和他人分离;人类可以和自然
分离。这种征服的态度前提就假定了有一个统治者,其他都是被统治
的对象"[8]。

二、劳伦斯性属哲学在作品中的发展变化

以上这些人生经历都分别被劳伦斯写入了他的小说和作品中,同
时也形成了他自己的哲学思想。尽管他从没写过一本哲学书,但他的
哲学思想却在他的作品中存在并发展着。他写道:

似乎对我来说,世界上最可悲的事情就是哲学和小说的分离。过
去,它们常常是一体的,就从神话时代开始……现在小说变得肤浅,哲
学变得抽象、枯燥。两者应该再次结合,结合于小说中[9]。

劳伦斯也确实是这样做的。为此,威廉姆斯(Williams)赞誉道,劳

伦斯"作为一个跨学科的思想家,作品游刃有余地穿梭于不同的文化形式中"[10]。他建议,要译读劳伦斯的文学作品或者哲学思想,读者们应该把两者结合,因为任何一方都是另一方的上下语境。

不难看出,要理解劳伦斯的作品,他的哲学思想是一根主线,贯穿于他的一系列作品中。关于他的哲学思想,许多学者都已经注意到劳伦斯喜欢用矛盾对立的观点陈述问题(Potter)[11]。在《意大利的暮色》(1916)一书中,劳伦斯就写道,"人的圆满有两面性,存在于自我(Self)和非自我(Selflessness)中"。其中"自我"指的是人的黑暗面,意识的底层,"创造性的无限"(Creative Infinite);"非自我"是指对自我的消灭,精神的主体,"不可逾越的无限"(Ultimate Infinite)。在《豪猪之死的反思》(1925)中,劳伦斯直接宣称了他的"双重性"原则,"我知道我是由两股流组成的,一股是短暂的,一股是永久的……在这两股对立的流—黑暗和光明的斗争和结合中形成了我。"他相信,"任何一切的本质都存在于两面性,甚至是一个石头"(qtd. in Dalski)[12]。对于劳伦斯来说,宇宙是按对立原则构成的。这些对立既斗争不断同时又是互补的。而且只要斗争和互补的因素存在,它们之间的对立平衡就一直持续。

可见,劳伦斯的双重性是他哲学思想的主要特色,也是他个人的主要特色。对于性属角色的理解,劳伦斯首先在《托马斯·哈代的研究》中就说道,"每一个男人在一开始就由男性和女性因素构成,其中男性因素总是努力占主导地位;而女人也如此,也是由男性和女性因素构成,女性因素占主导地位"[12]。他的这一概念非常类似于同时代女性作家伍尔夫所提的"双性同体"(androgyny)。

对于"双性同体",女性主义者内部是有争议的。萧瓦尔特认为,它"代表着男性特质与女性特质相对抗的一种逃避"[13]。陶丽·莫伊反对这一说法,认为"双性同体"意味着"女性主义者们的奋斗目标恰恰必须去解构男性特质和女性特质僵死的二元对立"[14]。时间验证了真理。随着性属研究的不断发展,人们普遍认可了性属角色由文化决定而不是由生理性别来决定。即,男性特质和女性特质是由后天文化环境决定的,与男性和女性的性别并无绝对先天绑定的关系。

因此作为 20 世纪的作家,劳伦斯和伍尔夫的这个思想可以说是合理、大胆、进步的,但他们受限于时代,似乎无法解释清楚这一现象,只能相信人们可以成为"男子气的女人或女子气的男人"(Showalter)[13]。在生活中,劳伦斯本人就非常喜欢做家庭主妇爱做的事,像煮饭、缝补和制衣(Moore)[15]。他还很腼腆,举止优雅、温柔,喜欢和女孩子呆在一起。许多评论家都指出,劳伦斯的小说一直都是在协调他自己体内的男性因素和女性因素。有些甚至认为,劳伦斯就是一个女人,如诺曼·梅勒和开罗·迪克斯就认为他是肉体上的男性,精神上的女性(qtd. in Baldick)[16]。

关于这一点,女性主义者们和其他男性评论家并不同意。因为纵观劳伦斯的整体作品,他都没有成功地协调好自己身上的男性因素和女性因素,也没有真正在为女性写作,相反刻意在作品中一步步地追求和确立男性的绝对意义。他不同阶段的作品和哲学思想可以证实这一点。

(一)早期和第二阶段——男孩思想到男人思想的转变

劳伦斯第一阶段的作品,《白孔雀》(1911)、《闯入者》(1912)和《儿子与情人》(1913)都是他早期有代表意义的作品。这些作品都不太成熟,仅仅展示了他年轻时的一些经历以及他和父母关系的一些问题。在这一阶段,劳伦斯只是一个"永远的妈妈男孩"(Ruderman)[17]。

但从《虹》(1915)的创作开始,劳伦斯就以自己的婚姻实例为蓝本,开始探讨男人和女人之间的关系,并建构出自己对此所持的哲学思想。他的妻子弗里达对他的创作影响至深。在他们相遇之时,她已是一个非常成熟和智性的已婚女子兼母亲。她曾与弗洛伊德信徒奥托·格罗斯交往甚密,相信"要是性是'自由'的,这个世界将直达天堂"(Frieda)[4]。在与劳伦斯私奔旅游时,她脱光所有衣服围着劳伦斯在房间里跳舞(Priest)[7]。年轻的劳伦斯被她开放的性行为所震惊。而这个场景也反复在他的小说《虹》《太阳》(1925,短篇小说)以及《查特莱夫人的情人》中出现。可以说,成熟、开放的弗里达使劳伦斯心理摆脱了对母亲不可自拔的迷恋。但弗里达事实上也和他母亲一样,是一个"公鸡般自负的女人"。矛盾的是他不但爱上了她还坚持和她结了婚。根据他的私人信件所说,他正是需要妻子的这种相异品性来引发他们之间的争吵,不然他会变得唯命是从,毁了他的写作天赋[6]。

很明显,劳伦斯的经历不但影响他的创作同时也影响到了他的哲学思想。在《虹》一书中,尽管劳伦斯提出了"二合一"(two in one)的婚姻观,但同时也感到女性存在的扩张对男性存在是种威胁。他认为,在婚姻中,如果男性在智性或精神上不能征服女性,男性至少在床上要满足她们。如果这一点做不到,反而女性在性上占了上风,那么男性也将彻底被毁灭。

因此为追求男性的完整或圆满,劳伦斯继续在《恋爱中的女人》(1920)探讨这一问题。在书中,他放弃了"二合一"的观点,提出"星际平衡"(stellar equilibrium)的理论,即"分离中的结合"(unison in separateness)。根据这一理论,男人和女人在性上从来不应该追求统治地位或利用对方的性作为意志工具,否则就犯了致命的错误;任何一方必须要打破自我的障碍,放弃所有个性并超越意识的局限。因为只有这样,双方中的个人才能保持完整的自我,完美地两极化。而当男性感到男子气得到确保,女性感到女子气得到确保,性行为就成为双方满足彼此最美妙的自我实现(Beauvoir)[18]。

波伏娃肯定了这一想法,认为"对于劳伦斯来说不是为了定义男女的特殊关系,而是为了使双方恢复生命的活力"[18]。然而,这一想法的实践在伯金和厄休拉的性关系中却无法令读者和有些批评家们信服。书中,劳伦斯对性采取的抽象和象征性描述令人困惑。杰弗里·米耶斯(Jeffrey Meyers)和威尔逊·耐特(Wilson Knight)就一直质疑伯金和厄休拉之间的性行为是"肛交"而不是正常的性交(qtd. in 高)[6]。事实上,正如波伏娃一语道破的,一方面劳伦斯提出男性的狂妄自大会激起女性的抵抗,只有双方毫无统治欲望的"相互的支配"(the reign of mutuality)才能达到完美的平衡;一方面他却没有构建出这样的支配,女主人公遵从了男主人公的想法,被他统治,被他拯救[18]。

(二)第三阶段——男性意义的极端

秉承第二阶段的思想,在这一阶段,劳伦斯进入了一个追求男性完整意义的极端。在作品《阿伦的拐杖》(1922),《袋鼠》(1923)和《羽蛇》(1926)中,我们可以看到男性都被创造成主角,都是男性世界的领导者;他们拒绝女性进入世界的权利;在个人关系上,都要求女性对男性绝对的服从。

大多学者都认为这一阶段是劳伦斯写作中最糟的部分,展现的是他在艺术创造上的下滑。事实上,这些作品完整地诠释了他在《无意识幻想》中所叙述的哲学思想—男权至上。对于这一部思想作品,Murry J. Middleton指出,劳伦斯想要解决的是自己的问题,亦或我们时代最大的难题——"如何重获性属的纯真",以及"改变男性世界,使未来没有孩子被培养成具有双重性、制约性,被迫成为他一样的人"[19]。此时的他已经放弃在《托马斯·哈代的研究》中所说的"双性同体",他认为:

"一个孩子在整个心智上要么男性,要么女性;体格上也是要么男性,要么女性。每一个活着的单细胞也是如此,这将持续至生命的终结。所以在男孩身上的每一个单细胞都是男性的,在女孩身上的每一个细胞都是女性的"[20]。

他相信,"至关重要的性两级"(vital sex polarity)才是"生命的动态魔力"(dynamic magic of life)[20]. 达拉斯基(Daleski)指出,这一阶段的思想是"劳伦斯本人一种严重的分裂"[12]。

这种分裂与他的人生经历密切相关。如前面所说,首先是他父母亲对他的影响,其次是他的妻子弗里达。再有,经历过第一次世界大战和见证一系列女权运动的爆发,他的分裂越发严重。原因在于,女性社会地位的日益提高和外出工作与男性的恐惧和地位的被动使他坚信,两性角色倒错,这对社会来说既不自然也不健康。这是一种"反常的过程"[20]。

为进一步解释男女性属的不同,他提出男人是积极的"思想家和行动家"而女人是被动的"情感爆发者"。他认为,当男人发现自己的情感来源于女人时,女人才通过男人学会如何思考,或者至少学会动脑子。他还给生活方方面面的男女角色下定义,提出不管是教育还是婚姻,男女角色在每一个方面都是不同的,这种不同应当在生活的早期阶段设立。他倡议,男孩和女孩应当分开教育、分别教育。女孩应当接受家庭艺术的教育而男孩则要教育成不同的个体。这种隔离教育的目的在于阻止女孩变得有"自我意识"(self-conscious),使她们只具备为家庭牺牲的意识;而男孩则能意识到他们的"男性统治"(manly rule)。在婚姻中,女人应当服从,男人则是占支配地位;女性的服从应当是"一种本能的、无意识的服从,发自无意识的忠诚"。除此外,劳伦斯还宣称,男人的世界是对外的,是处理深奥事物的;而"女人对于男人仅存在于黄昏……,傍晚和深夜才是她的"[20]。在他眼里,女人应该作为男人家里的性伴侣而存在。

达拉斯基从《托马斯·哈代的研究》,《无意识》和《凤凰》中整理出了劳伦斯对男性、女性的不同界定。他的这些界定可以让我们更好地了解他的思想。

男性(Male)	女性(Female)
动态(Activity)	静态;永恒(Stability,Immutability)
变化(Change)	永久,永恒(Permanence,Eternality)
动的意向(Will-to-Motion)	惰性的意向(Will-to-Inertia)
知识(Knowledge)	感觉,本能(Feeling,Nature)
不受时间影响(Timelessness)	此刻(The Moment)
思想(Idea)	肉体(Body)
做(Doing)	存在(Being)
抽象(Abstraction)	
公益事业(Public Good)	感官享受(Enjoyment through the Senses)
团体(Community)	
爱(Love)	法律(Law)
精神(Spirit)	灵魂(Soul)
意识(Consciousness)	感觉(Feelings)
理智(Mind)	感觉(Senses)
儿子(Son)	父亲(Father)
行动(Action)	感觉,情感(Feeling,Emotion)
茎(Stalk)	根(Root)
光(Light)	黑暗(Darkness)
向发现而动(Movement) towards discovery)	向起源而动(Movement towards origin)
抽象而机械的生活(Abstracted and Mechanical Life)	个性化的生活(Personal Life)
意志力中心群(Volitional Centres)	同情心中心群(Sympathetic Centres)

续表

男性(Male)	女性(Female)
权威(Authority)	温柔,充满同情心的角色(Gentle, All-Sympathetic Role)
主动(Active)	被动(Passive)
施动者(Initiator)	响应者(Responder)
说(Utterance)	情绪化(Emotion)
做并思考(Doing and Thinking)	生殖(Procreation)
决断(Assertion)	犹豫(Hesitation)
无肉体感觉的(Insentient)	敏感的 (Sensitive)
无惧、无情的英雄主义(Fearless, Relentless Heroism)	利他主义般的忍耐(Altruistic Endurance)
责任 (Responsibility)	温柔 (Tenderness)
无私、非家庭化(Disinterested, Non-Domestic)	
目标(Purpose)	感觉 (Feeling)
(*"The Duality of Lawrence"*)[12]	

从以上表格可以看出,劳伦斯积极地强调"男子气的绝对程度"(Daleski 11)[12]. 这些对男女性属特点的不同界定明显地以他想当然的男权思想为基础。对于他来说,男人和女人天生就是不同的。

但他的这种性属哲学非常不严谨,既形而上还自相矛盾。如:在女性原则中的"父亲"(Father)常会误导一些男性批评家,像霍夫先生就曾认为,"劳伦斯不是在建构双重性属模式的世界,例如'父亲'就和女性在同一边"(qtd. in Daleski)[12]。达拉斯基明确指出,"父亲"原则不过是劳伦斯"将女性价值观拟人化的一种上帝宣言"[12]。即,只要女性接受"父亲"这一原则,她们的思想和行为也将"无意识地忠实于"男性[20]。

除此外,他的"(通过)肉体(感知)"(knowing by "body")属于女性原则,却又和男性原则中的"(菲勒斯)意识"(phallic "conscious-ness")雷同。而他认为的男性原则,包括"抽象""精神""意志"或"思想"("abstraction","spirit","will","mind")却又是他一直在致力反对的。事实上,劳伦斯本人也承认他的想法经常是"动态"和"临时"的。正如布鲁斯特伯爵坦言,"当他敦促劳伦斯对他自己的哲学概念和心理学概念做一番文字表述时,劳伦斯摇摇头说:我将会在每一页中自相矛盾"(qtd. in Vivas)[21]。因此,连他自己都喊自己的哲学为"伪哲学"[20],也不足为奇了。

然而尽管劳伦斯的思想有其多变性和临时性的特点,这是事实,但他却一直坚持:男人和女人一直是相互对立,相互争斗却又互补的关系,就像(南北)两极。在回忆录《不是我,是风》中,他的妻子弗里达这样解释道:"(劳伦斯)认为任何一方都应该完整地保持自我的完整和独立,同时又像南北两极一样维持着一种相互依存的联系,由此将整个世界包揽在两者间。"[4]因此在男女双方的争斗关系上,如何"保持(男女关系的)平衡,不僭越、不倒坍"[4]一直是劳伦斯写作探讨的一大主题。

这一大主题确实能够粉饰劳伦斯的男权思想,正如辛普森(Simpson)一语道破,"从评论争议之初,对劳伦斯厌女症的攻击以及赞扬他对女性特质感性地描述,就一直并存"[22]。但他绝对不是一个平等主义者。科莫德(Kermode)指出,劳伦斯相信男人统治女人是自然的,如果反过来,女人统治了男人,那就是"身份认同危机"[23]。这也可以解释清楚为什么在他的哲学和写作中他对女性所具有的矛盾态度——一方面,他作为男性作家想要平衡男女之间的关系;一方面,他却无法纠正自己的男权思想,反而在作品中强调了这一点[24]。

(三)第四阶段——男性意义的延生

对男女关系的探讨,进入这一阶段,即劳伦斯创作的晚期,代表作非《查特莱夫人的情人》莫属。这部小说劳伦斯自 1926 年 11 月到 1928 年 1 月就 创作了三个版本,最终以最后一版广为流传。对于这一部小说,许多评论家都不承认是劳伦斯的代表作。作为支持者的里维斯(F. R. Leavis)就称这是"一部糟糕的小说",带有劳伦斯创作整体性的许多败笔[25]。埃利塞奥·维瓦斯(Eliseo Vivas)也批评这是一部艺术的失败品,他认为与前面作品相比,不过是"劳伦斯模仿了劳伦斯"[21]。然而,劳伦斯本人却把这部小说"高度视为他对这个世界的信息表达",因为他"允许自己在性交和爱情游戏的表述上享有高度自由"(Craig)[26]. 也正是这样的高度自由使得这部小说臭名昭著又威名远播。

在小说中,劳伦斯继续发展了他的双重哲学和男权思想。对于他来说,肉体已经被精神和意志牢牢掌控。这种枯燥、抽象、压抑的机械化精神生活已经毁灭了肉体和自我,导致人性和自然的分立。这些不和谐的关系又导致人的自我毁灭。为了保持生命的活力,他赞扬"血性意识"、"原始意识"或"菲勒斯意识",这可以解放真正的自我。因此,他主张要认识世界,肉体比意志更真实;对于保持人的生命力,"肉体接触","肉体劳动","肉体意识" 比意志更重要。简单地说,他相信,"肉体比意志更智慧"(Meyers)[27]。

因此,在小说中,他赤裸裸地描述了查特莱夫人康妮和其丈夫的看林人梅勒斯之间的性爱。将性视为大自然原始的生命力,是"大自然整体的灵魂所在"(Gregor)[28]。他自己也说,性就是生命、美和火。性爱的真实魅力在于"性的温暖和火热的交流过程"[3]146。性不丑陋,它可以带给人类"一种源源不断的附加能量和乐观"[3]148。通过肉体的性,康妮获得了重生,劳伦斯也在此基础上建构了"英格兰和白人种

族的重生"(Underset)[29]353这一伟大社会主题。威尔逊(Wilson)高度
赞誉道,"这是我长时间从英格兰看到的最鼓舞人心的书,……最棒的
写作之一",也是"他(劳伦斯)最有生命力和才气的书之一"[30]345。应
该说劳伦斯仅仅通过康妮的性重生就表达了人类灭亡—重生的崇高
主题,不得不说他是个天才。

也正因为这个崇高的主题,使得很多评论家忽视了劳伦斯男权思
想的延伸,而一再地"对劳伦斯的用辞累赘地复制和对他的预言仪式
般的复述"(Fernihough)[1]3。像里昂(Lyon)[31]和格雷戈尔(Gregor)[28]就坚持劳伦斯对性有特殊的理解,不是菲勒斯崇拜,而是对接
触和温柔的表达。是这样吗?

尽管劳伦斯在最后阶段放弃了第三阶段的极端表达,继续发展第
二阶段提出的"星际平衡"原则,让部分学者认为劳伦斯回到了研究男
女关系平衡的正轨。但劳伦斯最终并没有解决这个问题,越来越多的
评论家,如Daleski,Bedient,Rudikoff,Tindall和Squaires就指出小说
明显体现出了"康妮性爱的被动","女性意志的被放弃"和"梅勒斯上
帝般的权威"[12,32-35]。再者说,劳伦斯在这一阶段明确提出了"菲勒
斯婚姻"(phallic marriage)已说明了问题。波伏瓦在《第二性》中指
出,劳伦斯认为"菲勒斯是服务于两条河流结合的方式;它使这两种不
同的韵律结合成一条单独的流"[18]248。这种宣称展示了"男人不仅是
夫妻双方的一方,而且是他们结合的因素;他提供了双方的超越:'通
向未来的桥梁是阴茎'"[18]245。正是这一表述,劳伦斯将"性"等同于
"菲勒斯",证据已足够充分。很明显,他的目的是要巧妙地延续和再
创"男性的至高无上"。因此,为了解释宇宙间的性本质,他把对"大
地母亲的崇拜"替换成了"菲勒斯崇拜"[18]245-248。

波伏瓦继续指出,男主人公梅勒斯小说中的其他男主人公一样,
从一开始就掌握了智慧的秘密,这么久以来对宇宙的臣服已经完成,

他从中获得了很多内在的肯定,他似乎和任何一个骄傲的个人一样自大;这里有一个上帝在通过他说话:劳伦斯本人。小说中,女主人公"不是坏女人,她很好——却是被征服的"。"这种劳伦斯不得不提供给我们的'真实'女人的理想类型就是,一个毫无保留接受被定义为他者的女人"[18]245-254。

除了这部小说,劳伦斯晚期还在报刊杂志上发表了很多文章,表述自己对男人女人性属角色的观点。在《女人最好知道》(That Women Know Best)一文中,他指出女性应该照料孩子和整个家庭,男性的兴趣不在此[3]83-85。在《他自己屋子的主人》(Master In His Own House)一文中,他认为女性外出所从事的工作是男性不在乎的领域,男人在乎的领域是没有女性的侵扰的,"女人真正接管的不过是一场被(男人)放弃的战争"。他得出结论"男人必须做他自己屋子的主人"[3]99-101。在《母系氏族》一文中,他调侃道,男人被家庭牵制就被毁灭了,而女人即使被给予了作为母亲和大家长充分的独立和责任,当孩子冠上了母亲的姓,母亲也要照顾好这个姓[3]106。在《女人会变吗》,他认为女人应当如温柔的流,美丽、平静,而现代的"独立女性"不过是一些机器,"爱的机器","工作的机器","政治的机器","追求享受的机器"等等[3]153。在《公鸡般自负的女人和母鸡般温顺的男人》(Cocksure Women And Hen-sure Men)一文中,他明确指出现在的女人都表现得如男人一般,再怎么如公鸡般自负,她不过是只母鸡;再怎么追求投票权、福利、运动或事业,到头来,没有什么意义,因为母鸡的职责是下蛋[3]125-127。

像这些男权思想十足的论调还有很多。这些足以证明在晚期,劳伦斯并没有改变他的立场,他仍在追求男性意义的确定,并认为女性为追求平等所做的一切都是无稽之谈。他倡导女性要温柔和温顺地呆在家里,男人才是一家之主。他并未最终解决男女关系的平衡,也未如他在《查特莱夫人情人的申明》中所说的真正"为女性写作"（1929）[36]。他最后阶段的作品还是在为男权呐喊,尤其在经历了病魔折磨和男女主权之争后,他更迫切于男性意义的重新确立和延伸。

三、结论

劳伦斯是文学研究上最富争议的作家,其作品从四个阶段可以看出,虽有不同,但劳伦斯作为男性作家,在追求性属问题上,受父母失败婚姻的影响,也受自身婚姻和人生经历的影响,一直致力于研究男女关系平衡的主题,并创造性地用性来抽象表述其关系,最终其作品和思想深陷他自身经历的囹圄,还是没能客观和合理地解决这个问题,反而一步一步彰显了自己不平等的性属主张。从一开始对母亲的依恋和肯定,再到脱离母亲与女性的接触和思考,他对女性充满了好奇、探究,也带着恐慌、压力和保全男权传统意义的危机意识。因此,男女真正意义上的平等,性属的平等,在法律之外还有很长的路要走。男权意识的根深蒂固,时刻会威胁和颠覆性属平等取得的成果,我们还需继续努力奋斗,坚持和捍卫男女的平等。

参考文献:

［1］Fernihough Aanne, *D. H. Lawrence*［C］, Shanghai:Shanghai Foreign Language Education Press & Cambridge University Press,2003.

［2］Lawrence, D. H, *Studies in classic American literature*［M］, ed. by Seltzer, New-York ,1923:125.

［3］Lawrence, D. H. , *Late Essays And Articles*［C］, ed. by James T. Boulton, United Kingdom:Cambrige University Press,2004.

［4］Frieda,*Not I*,*But the Wind*［M］,New York:The Viking Press,1934:55,vii.

［5］Murray, B. "D(avid) H(erbert Richards) Lawrence"［C］. John Headley Rogers (ed.),*British Short-Fiction Writers*,1915–1945,Detroit:Gale Research,1996.

［6］高万隆:婚恋. 女权. 小说:哈代与劳伦斯小说的主题研究［M］,中国社会科

学出版社,2009:59,67,247.

[7] Priest, A M. "Married sex: Ann-Marie Priest highlights the importance of D. H. Lawrence as a proselytiser for the role of sex in love and marriage" [J] , *Meanjin* 66. 1 (2007):pp58 +.

[8]Sanders,R S. "Lady Chatterley's Loving and the Annihilation Impulse" [A] , in Laurie Di Mauro(ed.) , *Twentieth Century Literary Criticism*, Vol. 48 [C] , Gale Research Inc. 1993,pp134 – 140.

[9]Lawrence,D. H , *Phoenix: The Posthumous Papers of D. H. Lawrence* [M] , ed. By Edward D. McDonald,England:Penguin Books,1985:520.

[10]Williams,L R. *D. H. Lawrence* [M] , United Kingdom:Northcote House Publishers Ltd. ,1997:4 – 5.

[11]Potter ,S. *D. H. Lawrence:A First Study* [M] ,London:1930:24.

[12] Daleski, H. M , "The Duality of Lawrenc" [J] , *Modern Fiction Studies* 5. 1 (Spring1959) :3 – 18.

[13]Showalter E. "A Literature of Their Own" [C]. Zhu Gang(ed.) , *Twentieth Century Western Critical Theorie*, Shanghai:Shanghai Foreign Language Education Press,2001:241.

[14]Moi,Toril. ,"Sexual / Textual Politics" [C]. Zhu Gang(ed.) , *Twentieth Century Western Critical Theories*,Shanghai:Shanghai Foreign Language Education Press,2001:237.

[15]Moore O. "Further Reflections on the death of a Porcupine" [C] ,in *the Apple is Bibbten Again*,London n. d. :161.

[16]Baldick,Chris. , "Lawrence's Critical and Cultural legacy" [C]. Aanne Fernihough (ed.) , *D. H. Lawrence*, Shanghai: Shanghai Foreign Language Education Press & Cambridge University Press,2003:253 – 268.

[17]Ruderman,J. "Lawrence Among the Women:Wavering Boundaries in Women's Literary Traditions" [J] , *Studies in the Novel* 25. 2 (1993):249 +.

[18]Beauvoir de Simone, *The Second Sex* [M] , trans. by H Parshley, London:Vintage,1997.

[19]Murry J. Middleton, "The Nostalgia of D. H. Lawrence" [C]. Dennis Poupard

(ed), *Twentieth-Century Literary Criticism*, Vol. 9. Gale Research Inc. 1983:214 – 215.

[20]Lawrence,D. H,*Fantasia of the Unconscious and Psychoanalysis and the Unconscious*[M]. Great Britain:Penguin Books,1971:96,103,141,87 – 196,XIV.

[21]Vivas,E. *D. H. Lawrence:The Failure and the Triumph of Art*[M], Evanston: Northwestern University Press,1960:ix,3.

[22]Simpson,H. *D. H. Lawrence and Feminism*[M], Groom Helm Ltd,1982:13.

[23]Kermode,F. *Modern Essays*[C],London:Fontana Press,1990:155.

[24]杨文新.《木马赢家》中语言建构的隐含男权[J]. 重庆交通大学学报(社会科学版)2016(3):79 – 83.

[25]Leavis,F. R. ,*D. H. Lawrence:Novelist*. London,1955:94.

[26]Craig,Alec,*A History of the Conception of Literary Obscenity*[M], Cleveland, OH. :World Publishing,1963:146.

[27]Meyers,Jeffrey,*D. H. Lawrence and the Experience of Italy*[C]. Laurie DiMauro (ed),*Twentieth-Century Literary Criticism*,Vol. 48,Gale Research Inc. 1993:120 – 123.

[28]Gregor,Ian,"The Novel as Prophecy: 'Lady Chatterley's Lover' "(1962)[C]// Laurie Di Mauro (ed.), *Twentieth-Century Literary Criticism*, Vol. 48, Gale Research Inc. 1993:95 – 102.

[29]Undset,S. "D. H. Lawrence"[C]. Dedria Bryfonsk(ed.),*Twentieth-Century Literary Criticism*,Vol. 2,Gale Research Inc. 1979:353 – 354.

[30]Wilson,Edmund,"Sign of Life: ' Lady Chatterley's Lover"[C]. Dedria Bryfonsk (ed.),*Twentieth-Century Literary Criticism*,Vol. 2,Gale Research Inc. 1979:345.

[31]Lyon,J. M, " Lady Chatterley's Lover: Overview. "[C]// D. L. Kirkpatrick (ed.),*Reference Guide to English Literature*, Chicago:St. James Press,1991.

[32]Bedient,C. "The Radicalism of ' Lady Chatterley's Lover"(1966)[C]. Dedria Bryfonski and Sharon K. Hall(eds),*Twentieth-Century Literary Criticism*,Vol. 2,Gale Research Inc. 1979,pp370 – 371

[33] Rudikoff, S. " D. H. Lawrence and Our Life Today"[J], *Commentary*, 28 (1959):408 – 413.

[34]Tindall Y. W. "An Introduction to the Latter D. H. Lawrence". 1952. *Twentieth-*

Century Literary Criticism [M] . Dedria Bryfonski (eds) . Vol. 2. Gale Research Inc. 1979 : 356 – 357.

[35] Squires, M. "The Creation of Lady Chaterley's Lover" [C] . Laurie Di Mauro (ed.) , *Twentieth – Century Literary Criticism*, Vol. 48 , Gale Research Inc. 1993 , pp 129 – 134.

[36] Lawrence, D. II, "A Props of ' Lady Chatterley's Lover" [C] . Dennis Poupard (ed.) , *Twentieth-Century Literary Criticism*, Vol. 9 , Gale Research Inc. 1983 : 217 – 218.

（此文部分内容发表于《大理大学学报》2018 年第 3 期）

后 记

　　该研究从初稿成文到现在成书经历了 5 年时间。期间一直想用中文来发表，毕竟发表过的论文百分之九十都是中文，英文稿件也多译成中文发表。但为表示对我多年英语学习和研究的致敬和鞭策，最终决定以英文发表。文中有言语表达不当或失误的地方，欢迎大家批评和赐教，笔者不胜感激。

　　写作期间，在高职高专担任英语阅读教师时，涉及劳伦斯的短篇小说《木马赢家》。让学生课前准备展示，学生所收集的资料都是百度上谈到的对资本主义社会的过时批判。这些可以随意搜到的评论让学生先入为主地认为这一切都是资本主义社会造成的结果，而忽略了对社会人的责任思考。总的说来，学生对于评论文章的搜索和筛选过于拈轻怕重。另外，在课堂提问时，全班同学都认为保罗的死因是母亲不负责任而害死了儿子，对不在场的父亲和其他相关男性没有过多注意和追究责任。面对这样的认知局面，笔者深感人文素质教育的重要性和迫切性。我们的学生总体缺乏客观的自我评判，很容易跟随材料人云亦云，而性属平等在现实中实践起来真的是举步维艰。因此，笔者觉得有义务写篇文章为文中的母亲申辩，让学生了解性属平等的概念及对劳伦斯本人和作品的多方评论，为男女性属的平等贡献自己的微薄之力。

　　然而，一些高专院校的学生外国文学理论知识缺乏，人文素质教育不健全，缺乏主动、理智、客观和有深度的自我批评，这是事实也是现状。但高职学生也是社会的一大主力军，尽管高职学生的定位是技能性知识占主体，但英语精读和泛读的文章解读，不能简单地建立在理解文章语句、语法和作者主题思想上，也应当让学生了解不同视角的批评理论，从而树立正确的人生观、价值观和世界观；而不是感情用事、想当然，或者只会认为别人说的是对的，缺乏主见和思考，失去自我的性属平等权利和发展。

　　为此，笔者决定将该主题研究成果整理发表，呼吁性属平等教育的普及性和重要性。大家都认为，社会主义人人平等。但男女法律上的平等，却不等于意识和现实的平等。性别的歧视、就业上的歧视、发展上的不公平仍然存在。职业女性面临着来自工作、家庭、孩子的重重压力，而大多数男性却只顾自己的事业和个人发展，要求女性为家庭和孩子一味牺牲来达到所谓的对丈夫的"理解、支持和尊重"。事实上，不过是打着"一切为了家人"的大男子主义旗号，强调个人的利己主义。他们甚至认为这是真理，是自古至今的责任划分，从而让女性对婚姻和生活越来越失望，选择离婚，甚至不婚。

　　笔者在这个熔炉和围城里深有体会。性属平等不是简单的法律平等，要让人人意识到男女性属的平等，还需一代又一代人的努力和坚持。教育是首要的，只有从教育上着手，挖掉年轻一代人男权意识的根，再与有男权意识思想和行为的男人、女人据理力争，性属平等才有可能在法律之外的现实世界更早实现，男女的发展也才会在现实意义上更和谐、更公平、更合理，从而达到双赢的局面。

　　我们必须分清楚，男和女只是生理上的差别，生理上的男女性别与社会人的男女属性不是绝对的先天绑定。在社会上，你要如何发展,如何选择,应该是自由、公平、平等的,而不是女人该做什么,该是什么样;男人该做什么,该是什么样!和谐的社会,男人和女人应该互相理解、互相尊重、互相合作、互惠互利,平等地享受自己作为社会人的选择和权利。希望我们的社会越来越和谐,越来越公平,越来越合理,也越来越完美;不管男人、女人,都能自由地选择做真正的自己,而不是历代语言象征体系下有失偏颇的男权秩序下的那个自己。

The Principal Works of D. H. Lawrence

The White Peacock (novel)	1911
The Trespasser (novel)	1912
Love Poems and Others (poetry)	1913
Sons and Lovers (novel)	1913
The Prussian Officer (short stories)	1914
The Rainbow (novel)	1915
Amores (poetry)	1916
Twilight in Italy (essay)	1916
Look! We Have Come Through! (poetry)	1917
New Poems (poetry)	1918
The Lost Girl (novel)	1920
Women in Love (novel)	1920
Psychoanalysis and the Unconcious (essay)	1921
Sea and Sardinia (essays)	1921
Tortoises (Poetry)	1921
Aaron's Rod (novel)	1922
England, my England (short stories)	1922

Fantasia of the Unconcious (essay)   1922

Movements in European History (essays)   1922

Birds , Beasts and Flowers (poetry)   1923

Kangroo (novel)   1923

Studies in Classic American Literature (essays)   1923

Reflections on the Death of a Porcupine (essays)   1925

The Plumed Serpent (novel)   1926

Mornings in Mexico (essays)   1927

The Collected Poems of D. H. Lawrence. 2 vols. (poetry)1928

Lady Chtterley's Lover (novel)   1928 ①

The Woman Who Rode Away (shor stories)   1928

Pansies (poetry)   1929

The Escaped Cock (also published as *The Man Who Died* ,1931)

(novella)   1930

Love among the Haystacks (short stories)   1930

Nettles (poetry)   1930

The Virdin and the Gipsy (Novel)   1930

Etruscan Plaxes (essays)   1932

Last Poems (poetry)   1932

The Lovely Lady (short stories)   1933

The Ship of Death (poetry)   1933

A Modern Lover (short stories)   1934

The Spirit of the Plaxe (essays)   1935

Phoenix (essays and criticism)   1936

---

① three different versions , the other two were posthumously published : *The First Lady Chatterley* (novel) 1944 and *John Thomas and Lady Jane* (novel) 1972

Study of Thomas Hardy (essays and criticism)　　1936

Fire (Poetry)　　1940

The Complete Short Stories of D. H. Lawrance. 3 vols. (short stories)

　　1955

The Collected Letters of D. H. Lawrance. 2 vols. (letters)1962

The Complete Poems of D. H. Lawrence. 2vols. (poetry) 1964

The Complete Plays of D. H. Lawrence (drama)　　1966

Phoenix II (essays and criticism)　　1968

Late Essays and Articles(essays)　　2004